"Mommy, look who came to visit,"

Hannah said. "Mr. Man is here."

Caleb McMann, Erica's own personal version of Mr. Rogers in the neighborhood, stood holding a tray with three tall glasses of pink lemonade.

However, Mr. Rogers would never appear shirtless, nor would he look as good as Caleb did at the moment. Caleb, with his expanse of tanned, muscled chest and a flirtatious smattering of dark chest hair, banished all pretense of relaxation.

This man is dangerous, a tiny voice whispered in the back of her head. He was temptation to all the things Erica had put behind her, all the emotions she'd sworn she'd never feel again. He was a man to be avoided at all costs.

What was he doing here? Why did he seem so intent on being friendly with her, popping in and out of her house, fixing sinks, building tree houses, bearing doughnuts and lemonade?

What did he want from her?

Dear Reader,

Once again Intimate Moments is offering you six exciting and romantic reading choices, starting with *Rogue's Reform* by perennial reader favorite Marilyn Pappano. This latest title in her popular HEARTBREAK CANYON miniseries features a hero who'd spent his life courting trouble—until he found himself courting the lovely woman carrying his child after one night of unforgettable passion.

Award-winner Kathleen Creighton goes back INTO THE HEARTLAND with *The Cowboy's Hidden Agenda,* a compelling tale of secret identity and kidnapping— and an irresistible hero by the name of Johnny Bronco. Carla Cassidy's *In a Heartbeat* will have you smiling through tears. In other words, it provides a perfect emotional experience. In *Anything for Her Marriage,* Karen Templeton proves why readers look forward to her books, telling a tale of a pregnant bride, a marriage of convenience and love that knows no limits. With *Every Little Thing* Linda Winstead Jones makes a return to the line, offering a romantic and suspenseful pairing of opposites. Finally, welcome Linda Castillo, who debuts with *Remember the Night*. You'll certainly remember her and be looking forward to her return.

Enjoy—and come back next month for still more of the best and most exciting romantic reading around, available every month only in Silhouette Intimate Moments.

Yours,

Leslie Wainger

Leslie J. Wainger
Executive Senior Editor

Please address questions and book requests to:
Silhouette Reader Service
U.S.: 3010 Walden Ave., P.O. Box 1325, Buffalo, NY 14269
Canadian: P.O. Box 609, Fort Erie, Ont. L2A 5X3

IN A HEARTBEAT
CARLA CASSIDY

Silhouette®
INTIMATE™ MOMENTS®

Published by Silhouette Books

America's Publisher of Contemporary Romance

This book is dedicated to my mother,
who, despite her own heart condition,
has lived her life with courage and humor
and has filled my life with love.
Thanks, Mom,
for being a woman I not only love
but also admire with all my heart.

 SILHOUETTE BOOKS

ISBN 0-373-27075-5

IN A HEARTBEAT

Copyright © 2000 by Carla Bracale

This edition published by arrangement with Harlequin Books S.A.

Visit Silhouette at www.eHarlequin.com

Printed in U.S.A.

Books by Carla Cassidy

CARLA CASSIDY

is an award-winning author who has written over thirty-five books for Silhouette. In 1995 she won Best Silhouette Romance from *Romantic Times Magazine* for *Anything for Danny*. In 1998 she also won a Career Achievement Award from *Romantic Times Magazine* for Best Innovative series.

Carla believes the only thing better than curling up with a good book to read is sitting down at the computer with a good story to write. She's looking forward to writing many more books and bringing hours of pleasure to readers.

IT'S OUR 20th ANNIVERSARY!
We'll be celebrating all year,
Continuing with these fabulous titles,
On sale in May 2000.

Romance

#1444 Mercenary's Woman
Diana Palmer

#1445 Too Hard To Handle
Rita Rainville

#1446 A Royal Mission
Elizabeth August

#1447 Tall, Strong & Cool Under Fire
Marie Ferrarella

#1448 Hannah Gets a Husband
Julianna Morris

#1449 Her Sister's Child
Lilian Darcy

Desire

#1291 Dr. Irresistible
Elizabeth Bevarly

#1292 Expecting His Child
Leanne Banks

#1293 In His Loving Arms
Cindy Gerard

#1294 Sheikh's Honor
Alexandra Sellers

#1295 The Baby Bonus
Metsy Hingle

#1296 Did You Say Married?!
Kathie DeNosky

Intimate Moments

#1003 Rogue's Reform
Marilyn Pappano

#1004 The Cowboy's Hidden Agenda
Kathleen Creighton

#1005 In a Heartbeat
Carla Cassidy

#1006 Anything for Her Marriage
Karen Templeton

#1007 Every Little Thing
Linda Winstead Jones

#1008 Remember the Night
Linda Castillo

Special Edition

#1321 The Kincaid Bride
Jackie Merritt

#1322 The Millionaire She Married
Christine Rimmer

#1323 Warrior's Embrace
Peggy Webb

#1324 The Sheik's Arranged Marriage
Susan Mallery

#1325 Sullivan's Child
Gail Link

#1326 Wild Mustang
Jane Toombs

Prologue

"**M**r. McMann! Wait."

Caleb turned to see the doorman hurrying toward him, a large package in the man's arms. "Evening, Ricky," Caleb replied.

The young man flashed Caleb a friendly smile. "How you doing, sir? Haven't seen you around much these past few months."

"I've been doing a lot of traveling. But, as always, it's good to get home." Caleb punched the elevator button.

"It's nice to have you back." Ricky held out the package. "This came for you today."

"Thanks." The elevator dinged and the door swooshed open. With a parting nod to Ricky, Caleb stepped into the elevator and pressed the button that would take him to his penthouse apartment.

As the elevator carried him up, he looked at the return label on the brown wrapped package. It was from his aunt Fanny. He groaned inwardly. No telling what it contained.

Old age had given Fanny a dose of senility marked by occasional moments of semi-clarity. And in those moments she often sent a gift to her favorite nephew. Sometimes extravagant, sometimes inexpensive, the gifts were almost always utterly useless and often just plain odd.

He shifted the package from one arm to the other as he unlocked his apartment door. There was no sense of welcome as he entered the elegant suite. He'd lived here for almost nine months, but had done almost nothing to make the place his own. It was as sterile and impersonal as the hotel rooms he stayed in while traveling.

He tossed the package on the sofa, then went into the kitchen and grabbed a beer from the refrigerator. As he walked back toward the living room he loosened his tie and unbuttoned his shirt collar.

Sinking onto the sofa, he opened his beer, took a deep swallow, then leaned back and sighed in exhaustion. It felt as if he'd been on the run forever, looking over building sites, supervising construction, fighting with zoning commissions, and cursing inclement weather conditions.

He had huge jobs going on in a dozen states, had

made more money in the last year than he'd ever spend in his lifetime. But tonight, he was just plain tired…tired of flights, tired of strange motel rooms, tired of work and all the hassles that came with being the owner of a multimillion-dollar construction company.

He finished his beer and returned to the kitchen for a second one. The empty apartment seemed to close in on him, and the silence became suffocating.

Back on the sofa he jabbed the button on the remote to turn on the television, welcoming the white noise that filled the stifling void.

Twisting off the top of the new beer, he eyed the package next to him, trying to guess what Fanny might have sent him. Her last gift had been an ashtray in the shape of a football stadium. Caleb had never smoked in his life.

He set his beer on the coffee table and picked up the package. It took him only seconds to rip away the brown wrapping paper and reveal a plain white oblong box. He pulled off the lid and gently shoved aside the pale pink tissue paper.

His breath hissed inward as he stared at the porcelain-faced, ruffle-clad doll with painted features and long, golden curls. Scarcely breathing, Caleb picked up the card that rested near the doll's feet.

A birthday card.

For Katie.

Katie Rose McMann's birthday was in two days. She would have been seven.

If she hadn't died.

His crazy aunt Fanny had remembered Katie's birthday, but had somehow forgotten that she'd passed away nine months before.

A burst of laughter exploded from Caleb's lips, hysterical laughter that turned into a deep, wrenching sob.

He swallowed against it, fighting for control. He'd done so well. For the past nine months he'd managed to keep command over his emotions, but he felt his control slipping away as another sob choked in his throat.

He stood abruptly, the doll sliding from his lap, banging into the table and tipping over his beer bottle. He had to go…had to escape…had to get away from the dark despair that suddenly blinded him, threatened to paralyze him…threatened to consume him.

Katie. Her name reverberated in his brain, bringing with it a vision of her beloved face. That funny little grin, those bright blue eyes, the mop of golden curls and the chubby cheeks that made her appear half cherub, half pixie.

He stumbled to the French doors that led out onto a balcony. Air. He needed air. God…he couldn't breathe. Why couldn't he breathe? What was wrong with him?

But he knew. Grief. He'd been running away from it for the last nine months, but now it had found him. It ripped at him, tore at his insides and he gripped his head with his hands as inchoate moans escaped him.

He stepped outside into the cool air. "Katie." Her name began as a wail, then swelled inside him until he was screaming it over and over again, sobs shaking him as the night wind blew the sound of her name away.

He screamed her name until it was nothing more than a hoarse whisper of anguish. If only he hadn't been in such a hurry that day. If only he'd made certain her seat belt was fastened. If only he'd been able to evade the truck that appeared out of nowhere and slammed into their car. But all the if-onlys in the world didn't matter now. Katie was gone and nothing would ever bring her back again.

Carelessness had killed her. The carelessness of a tired truck driver, and Caleb's own negligence had killed his baby girl.

He crumbled to the ground, his head bowed to his knees as tears blinded him. Never again would he hold her in his arms, smell the sweet scent of sunshine and bubble bath.

Never again would he see that special little smile, hear the childish giggles that had always made him grin despite his mood. And never again would he feel her warm little arms around his neck, hear her whisper in that beloved young voice, "I love you, Daddy Doodle."

Grief could kill a man. Caleb knew he had to be dying. The pain in his heart was too great to bear, the emptiness in his soul too abysmal to survive.

It was said that people were never given more burdens than they could handle…but somewhere a mistake had been made. There had been too much loss in Caleb's life. He'd grieved when his wife had died five years ago, but the grief had been necessarily short-lived. He'd had two-year-old Katie to raise, to nurture and love.

But this…this loss of his child was too much to bear. He wasn't strong enough for this. How was he supposed to continue existing without the little girl who'd been his world, his life, his heart?

He had no idea how long he remained on the balcony. He cried until there were no more tears, cursed until there were no more words, and finally there was nothing left inside him except a chilling bleakness, an excruciating emptiness.

Wearily, not knowing how to go on, yet not knowing how not to, he pulled himself up and stumbled back into the apartment.

Depleted of energy, drained of emotion, he picked up the box containing the doll that had been the catalyst for his grief and placed the lid back on it. He uprighted the fallen beer bottle and sank onto the sofa.

His eyes felt gritty and his throat burned, but these were only mild discomforts compared to the pain in his heart. He could build enormous buildings, take raw wood and construct beautiful, lasting furniture, but he didn't know how to piece his soul back together.

Dully, he stared at the television, where the late-night news was just winding down.

"And we end our newscast tonight with a happy story," the perky blond announcer exclaimed. "Last week we brought you the story of sixteen-year-old Maria Lomax, who'd been blind since birth. Tonight, Maria can see, thanks to a miracle of modern medicine and through the generosity of a very special couple."

The announcer's picture disappeared and the screen filled with a picture of a hospital room where a lovely young girl was crying and hugging an older couple.

"John and Linda Corral lost their son a week ago to a motorcycle accident," the female narrator continued. "But, in donating their son's corneas, they gave the gift of sight to Maria, who can now see. Earlier this afternoon the couple met with Maria. John and Linda said the meeting provided the closure and healing they desperately needed, and they encourage everyone to consider organ donation."

Closure and healing. Caleb's mind worked to wrap around the concept behind those two words. It seemed impossible to comprehend while the agony of loss still encased him. Yet was it possible to find closure and healing? Was it possible to get past the pain that now debilitated him?

He squeezed his eyes tightly closed, drawing in deep, uneven gulps of air. There was no going back now. The floodgates of his grief had been opened by the arrival of the doll and he knew now that no matter how far he traveled, no matter how fast he ran, his grief would be inside him, consuming him.

He opened his eyes as a surge of energy ripped through him. For his own sanity and survival, it was time to look for his own healing, his own closure. And that's exactly what he intended to do.

Chapter 1

She stood in her backyard, tossing a big, colorful ball up in the air, then catching it. Although she pretended to be interested solely in her game of catch, Caleb felt her gaze lingering on him with interest.

It had been the same for the past three days. Each afternoon, the little girl came out to play. The first day, she'd remained close to her house, eyeing him across the distance of her yard and his.

The second afternoon, she'd moved to the center of her yard, playing with the ball and watching Caleb as he worked to replace the rotten railings on the porch of his new home.

Today, she was playing near the fence that separated the two properties, and Caleb had a feeling this time she would talk to him.

The thought of connecting with her filled him with incredible anticipation and an equal amount of dread. Everything he'd done in the past month had been in the hope of making contact with Hannah Marie Clemmons.

When he'd arrived in St. Louis two weeks ago, he'd rented a motel room, only intending to drive by the house where she lived, hoping to see her alive and well, playing like any other normal, healthy five-year-old. He'd thought that would be enough.

It wasn't.

It had been on one of his drive-bys that he'd noticed the big old two-story house next to the one where the little girl lived, was for sale. His reasons for buying it were twofold. First and foremost, it offered immediate proximity to Hannah. Secondly, his hands had itched to turn the handyman's nightmare into something regal and wonderful again. In the past year, he'd gotten so caught up in the running of his business, he'd forgotten how much he loved to build...to do the physical labor of transformation.

He'd needed a vacation from the business, had needed to get back to what he loved. And this house, neglected and in total disrepair, offered such an opportunity. He figured he'd renovate the house, and sell it when he decided it was time to return to his life in Chicago.

"Hey, mister."

Caleb looked up from the four-by-six he'd been measuring.

She stood at the fence. "Could you get my ball?" She pointed to the ball, which rested near where he'd been working.

"Sure." Caleb's fingers trembled as he picked up the bright red globe. This would be his first, really up-close look at her. He walked to where she stood at the fence.

Brown eyes. He'd hoped they'd be blue…as blue as the spring sky overhead…as blue as his Katie's. Hannah was a pretty little girl, with gamine features framed by a curtain of long, dark hair. The utter antithesis of blond-haired, blue-eyed Katie.

As he handed her the ball, the familiar weight of grief crushed against his chest. What he wanted to do was scoop her up in his arms, breathe deeply into her hair, see if she smelled like Katie…that wonderful blend of sunshine and little girl.

"Thank you," she said with a bright smile, then she turned and ran back toward the tiny house where Caleb knew she lived with her mother.

The agony inside his chest expanded as he watched her go. The little girl who lived because his little girl had died.

Caleb wasn't sure what he'd been expecting, but it wasn't the renewal of the anguish of loss. He stumbled through the back door of the house, half-blinded by tears he'd thought he no longer had the capacity to cry. Sinking into a chair at the table, he drew in deep, steadying breaths, wondering if this all wasn't an incredible mistake on his part.

He hadn't realized it would be so hard. Where was the healing, the closure he'd come here to find? Maybe his expectations had been too high. After all, grief was a long process. Surely he couldn't expect to be healed by a single meeting with Hannah.

Time. That was what he needed. Time to get to know Hannah, who was forever bound to him through a miracle of modern medicine.

He didn't want to tell Hannah or her mother about his connection to them. His grief was private, and far too big a burden for them to bear.

He'd come here to meet them with two goals in mind. The first was his need to witness that Hannah Clemmons's life was good, that she had all the things he'd ever wanted Katie to have.

The second reason was his longing to find out what the heart remembered. When the doctors had taken Katie's heart and placed it into Hannah's chest, had any memories been transferred, did pieces of Katie's soul somehow migrate into Hannah? He knew the very idea was probably crazy, but it was a hope he hadn't been able to let go of until he discovered the truth for himself.

The next afternoon he was once again working on the porch when Hannah came out into her backyard. She didn't even pretend to be playing catch, but rather walked right up to the fence and offered him a sunny smile.

"Did you buy that house?" she asked.

Caleb nodded. "I sure did."

"It's a wreck," she said with childish candor.

He smiled. "Yes, it is. But, I'm fixing it."

"It's a big house. It's gonna take lots of fixing." She smiled again. "What's your name?"

"Caleb. Caleb McMann."

"I'm Hannah. Hannah Marie Clemmons. And my mommy's name is Erica."

Caleb walked over to where she stood at the fence. Just like yesterday he felt a curious mix of interest and anxiety. "It's very nice to meet you, Miss Hannah."

She giggled, and the sound of girlish joy wrapped around Caleb's heart and squeezed painfully tight. Did all little-girl laughter hold that special timbre of gaiety, that sense of utter elation?

She sobered and eyed him curiously. "Are you going to build a tree house in that tree?" She pointed to the old oak that towered over his backyard.

Caleb tilted his head and looked speculatively at the tree. "Now that you mention it, those thick limbs make a perfect place for a little tree house, don't they?"

Hannah nodded. "One with real windows and pink curtains, and you'd let me come over and play in it anytime I wanted."

A burst of laughter erupted from Caleb, surprising him. Maybe he *would* build her that tree house she dreamed of. After all, he had time on his hands and it would obviously make Hannah happy. And that was what this was all about, right? It had been almost a year since he'd had anything to laugh about. It felt good…natural.

"Hannah."

They both looked toward Hannah's house, where a young woman stepped out the back door. The first thing Caleb noticed about her was her hair, a long curtain of dark strands that gleamed with red highlights in the afternoon light.

"That's my mommy," Hannah explained.

As the woman drew closer, Caleb saw the immediate physical resemblance between mother and daughter. Like Hannah, Erica Clemmons had petite features and large eyes, only unlike Hannah's, Erica's were the blue of a summer's day.

"Hannah, you shouldn't be bothering people," she admonished as she approached.

"I'm not bothering people," Hannah protested. "I'm just talking to Mr. Man."

"Hi. Caleb McMann." Caleb held his hand out over the top of the fence.

She hesitated a moment, then shook the hand he offered. "Erica Clemmons." She dropped her hand and placed it on Hannah's shoulder. "I hope she hasn't been bothering you."

"Not at all," he said hurriedly. He smiled at Hannah. "She's been very neighborly."

Erica looked at his tools strewn about, then at the towering house. "Looks like you've got your work cut out for you," she observed.

"Yeah. It's going to take a lot of time, but it's mostly cosmetic. The structure is sound."

"Mommy said if she had a million dollars she'd buy that house," Hannah quipped.

Erica blushed and Caleb realized she was quite pretty. "If I had a million dollars, I'd do a lot of things, sweetheart." She turned and Caleb knew she was about to leave. He didn't want her to go...not yet.

"I'll bet your place used to be a part of this house," he said.

She looked at the small structure she and Hannah called home. "I think somebody told me at one time that it used to be the carriage house of your place...or maybe it was the gardener's cottage."

Once again she placed a hand on Hannah's shoulder. "It's time for you to come inside." She looked at Caleb. "Good luck with your work, Mr. McMann."

"Thanks." Caleb watched them go, his heart thudding wildly in his chest. He wasn't sure what he wanted...what he needed. But he knew his brief interaction with both Hannah and her mother wasn't enough.

"Belinda says her mommy lets her stay up until real late, and she gets to go to bed whenever she wants," Hannah complained when her mother told her it was bath and bedtime.

"Belinda is older than you," Erica reminded her. "And Belinda is full of beans."

Hannah giggled. "What kind of beans?"

"Lima beans." Erica laughed as her daughter's face wrinkled in disgust.

"Hi, Peaches." Hannah greeted the apricot poodle who bounded across the kitchen floor, her toenails clicking across the linoleum. She scooped up the dog and laughed as a little pink tongue licked her cheek. "Peaches doesn't want me to take a bath. She wants me to play with her." Hannah looked up at her mother with big brown, appealing eyes.

"Oh, no you don't." Erica took the dog from Hannah's arms. "You aren't about to get out of taking a bath." She put Peaches on the floor and the poodle instantly sought refuge beneath the table, obviously thinking the bath was for her.

They went into the bathroom, where Erica started the water in the tub while Hannah undressed. "Lots of bubbles," she commanded, watching like a miniature drill sergeant as her mother fixed the water to her liking.

Once Hannah was happily ensconced amid the bubbles and warm water, Erica left the bathroom, knowing her daughter would dawdle, playing with bath toys until the water cooled.

Walking back into the kitchen, Erica silently listed all the errands she needed to run the next day. Before she got halfway through them, she was mentally exhausted. It seemed like exhaustion had been a part of her life forever, but more so lately than ever before.

It was odd. She'd functioned so well for so long,

and now that Hannah was finally relatively healthy, Erica felt particularly fragile.

She poured herself a cup of coffee, gave Peaches a biscuit, then stood at the kitchen sink. Peering out the window that offered a view of the house next door, she fought against the sadness of another dream lost.

She'd hoped the big old house would remain empty until she could afford to buy it. It had been a silly, unrealistic dream. She owed enough money that she and Hannah would probably never live in a house that had their names on the deed.

Caleb McMann. She thought of the man who'd bought her dream house. Nice-looking man. With his dark hair and blue eyes, those wide shoulders and lean hips, he was what Sherry would call a hunk. Probably a very married hunk, she thought. Not that she cared.

With a rueful smile, she turned away from the window and went back into her bedroom. Yes, he was probably married and had a half dozen kids. It would be nice if one of them were Hannah's age. Friendships had been difficult while she'd been ill, and no children her age lived in the neighborhood.

"Mommy, I'm done."

Erica set her cup down on the counter and hurried back into the bathroom. Grabbing a thick, fluffy towel from the linen closet, she opened it wide to welcome the wet, sweet-smelling child.

"Hmm, you smell like a giant, ripe strawberry," Erica exclaimed, rubbing Hannah dry as she giggled and wiggled like an eel. "Now, let me see your boo-boo."

Hannah stood still as Erica gazed at the scar that bisected her little chest. Every day it seemed to fade just a bit more. "It's looking good, munchkin."

Hannah nodded solemnly. "But it will never, ever go away."

It was a nightly routine, one they had begun almost ten months before, right after Hannah's lifesaving surgery. "No, it will never, ever go away completely." Erica kissed the puckered skin. "But, it's the best kind of boo-boo to have. Now you have a new strong, special heart." Erica knocked on her daughter's chest. "Hello in there."

Hannah giggled as Erica tickled her ribs. "You're silly, Mommy."

"I am, and your silly mommy says to scoot into your room and get your pajamas on and get into bed." She smiled as her daughter ran naked down the hall-way and disappeared into her bedroom.

It was hard to believe that in just a couple of weeks Hannah would be six years old. There were times when it seemed like she'd been born only yesterday, and other times when it seemed an eternity ago. She took the towel and swiped at the bubble-bath residue on the sides of the tub.

Six years. All thanks to a miracle of modern science. Erica intended to have a huge party, bigger than any Hannah had ever celebrated before. It would be one of the few birthdays Hannah hadn't spent in a hospital room.

"Okay Mommy, come tuck me in."

Tossing the towel into the hamper, Erica hurried into the small bedroom where Hannah was already beneath the colorful sheet on the bed. "Before you tell me good-night, you have to say good-night to Harry," Hannah commanded.

Erica groaned. She hated Harry. But she loved Hannah, and so walked across the room to the hamster cage and leaned down to tap on the glass. "Good night, Harry," she said to the gray hamster who poked his head out of a pile of pine shavings and wiggled his nose in greeting.

"He says good-night and he loves you," Hannah interpreted.

"Oh good, I'll sleep much better tonight knowing Harry loves me." Erica sat down on the edge of the bed. "But I'd sleep wonderfully better with a Hannah hug."

With a grin, Hannah reached up and hugged her mom around her neck. Erica returned the embrace, her heart swelling with her intense love for the child. At the quick, immediate sting of tears, she realized again how fragile she was, how afraid she was to hope that finally the fears for Hannah's very life were behind them and only normal childhood experiences lay ahead.

"Mommy?"

"What, sweetie?" Erica sat on the edge of the mattress and stroked Hannah's dark hair.

"I liked Mr. Man. He has daddy eyes."

"Daddy eyes?" Erica frowned. She distinctly remembered Caleb McMann's eyes. Sharp blue, with a slight silvery shine that was in direct contrast to his dark hair.

"Yeah, you know, all shiny and smiley and nice. Daddy eyes."

Erica smoothed her daughter's hair one last time, then stood. "It's time for little brown eyes to go to sleep. Good night, munchkin." She kissed Hannah's forehead, then tucked the sheet beneath her chin. "Sleep tight."

As Hannah murmured a drowsy reply, Erica turned off the light but hesitated at the door.

She smiled as her gaze lingered on the sleeping child. Peaches padded into the room and curled up on the dog bed in the corner, but the act didn't fool Erica one bit. She knew the moment she moved away from the door, Peaches would jump up in the bed with Hannah.

Leaving the bedroom, Erica went into the kitchen and refilled her coffee cup, her daughter consuming her thoughts.

Born with a malfunctioning heart, Hannah had been a weak, frail child whom the doctors had said would not live to see her first birthday. But Hannah had been a fighter, and defying the odds seemed to be her specialty. Hannah's father, Chuck, had stuck through the first year with the sickly baby, but eventually he'd left, incapable of dealing with the situation.

She sipped her coffee, realizing she'd finally managed to get beyond the hurt and betrayal Chuck had left behind. He was the loser. He'd missed out on so much.

Smiling, she sat down at the kitchen table. Hannah might not have been given a good heart at the beginning of her life, but she'd been blessed with the spirit of a warrior. Courageous and brave, she also possessed a loving, optimistic attitude that often awed and humbled her mother.

Yes, her ex-husband had been the loser. Oh, he'd escaped the frantic worry, the enormous debt left by medical bills. He'd run from the responsibility and the fear of raising an ill child, but he'd lost out on the wondrous gift of knowing...and loving Hannah.

"Daddy eyes."

Lately, Hannah had become obsessed with the idea of a daddy. It was as if now that her heart was fixed, she felt the empty space that her father had left when he'd abandoned her.

The phone rang, the shrill sound splintering the silence of the house. Erica jumped up from the table and grabbed for the receiver, not wanting the unexpected noise to awaken Hannah.

"Hey girl, what's going on?"

Erica settled back in her chair, warmth suffusing her at the sound of her best friend's voice. "Hi, Sherry. Not much going on here. I just put Hannah to bed and

I'm relaxing for a few minutes before I follow her example.''

"Good grief, Erica. It's just a few minutes after nine on a Saturday night," Sherry protested. "Hon, you definitely need to get a life."

Erica laughed. "I have a life. It's just not as exciting as yours."

"Compared to yours, a monk's life would be exciting," Sherry retorted dryly. "And that's why I'm calling. I'm having a little dinner party next Friday night and..."

"No," Erica interrupted.

"You haven't even heard me out yet."

"I heard you last week, and the week before that. You've got to stop trying to fix me up with men. I'm not interested."

There was a long pause from Sherry. "Erica, Hannah's last operation was almost a year ago. She's doing terrific, getting healthier every day. It's time for you to stop worrying so much about her and start thinking of your own happiness. It won't hurt to leave her with a baby-sitter for the evening."

"I'm happy," Erica interjected. She rubbed her forehead, where a headache danced light fingers of pain across her brow.

Sherry sighed impatiently. "You can't be happy. You're alone."

Again Erica laughed. "Contrary to popular belief, some women can be happy without a man in their life. Besides, I'm not alone. I have Hannah."

Again there was a long pause and Erica sighed, knowing the pause didn't indicate Sherry was giving up, only that she was regrouping. "Don't you ever miss it?" she finally asked.

Erica frowned, again rubbing her forehead. "Miss what?"

"Sex." Sherry sighed impatiently. "I know it's been a long time, Erica, but surely you remember sex."

Erica's headache intensified. "Sherry, I refuse to have this discussion."

"Ah, the ice maiden has appeared, hiding behind that cold exterior that keeps people at bay."

Erica said nothing, silently admitting that Sherry knew her only too well.

"Erica, I worry about you. You work at home, you don't go out. You don't allow anyone in your life. You keep yourself so isolated from others."

Sherry sighed. "Okay, I'll stop now. I know this lecture is having about as much of an effect on you as a raindrop in the ocean. Are we on in the morning?"

"Sure," Erica agreed. It was customary for the two friends to share coffee early every Sunday morning. "I'll see you then."

After hanging up, Erica shut off the coffeemaker, thinking of the woman who had been her best friend since they had been freshmen in high school.

However, as close as the two women had been over

the years, their life-styles were far too different for Sherry to ever understand Erica.

Sherry Burnett had been raised in a loving, supportive family, and five years ago had married a wonderful man who adored her. She and her husband, David, had decided not to have children. David was a high-powered lawyer, and Sherry enjoyed an exciting job as an investigative reporter for an alternative newspaper in town.

Sherry was smart and savvy, but she didn't understand loving a child. She couldn't understand the commitment of a mother to a child in need.

After shutting off the kitchen light, Erica checked on Hannah—who slept peacefully with Peaches curled up next to her—then went into her small bedroom.

As she undressed and got ready for bed, her thoughts raced. Unlike so many of Erica's friends, who'd drifted away, not knowing what to say, unable to deal with Erica's grief and Chuck's anger over Hannah's heart condition, Sherry had remained the one constant source of support Erica so desperately needed.

She pulled her nightgown over her head and turned out her light. In the faint illumination filtering through the curtains from the street lamp out front, she crawled into bed.

Sherry's question came back to haunt her.

"Don't you ever miss it?"

Well, she could honestly say she never gave much

thought to sex. She didn't have the time or the energy to think about it.

However, if she were perfectly honest with herself, she'd admit that she did miss somebody holding her through the night. She missed the lingering scent of cologne on the pillow next to hers, the warmth of shared body heat on a cold, wintry night. But she could always buy a bottle of men's cologne and an electric blanket would take care of her cold feet.

Erica had learned her lesson well. First from her father, who had walked out on them when Erica had been twelve, then from Chuck.

Men were great when the good times rolled. But, when trouble reared its ugly head, when the road of life got bumpy, men cut their losses and ran. Erica now knew that she only had herself to depend on.

No, she didn't need a man, or anyone else in her life. Not in any way, shape or form. She just needed Hannah, and Hannah needed her. They were a unit, a family. She wasn't willing to ever open her heart again to any male.

She'd done everything she could for the past six years to heal and protect Hannah. She wasn't about to bring a man into their lives. She wasn't about to allow a man to ever again steal a piece of their hearts, then ride off into the sunset without them.

Chapter 2

"Mr. Brown, you promised me you'd have somebody come over and look at this sink a month ago." Erica held the phone in one hand and frantically removed the full pan of water from beneath the leaking pipe, quickly exchanging it for an empty pan.

What she wanted to do was reach through the phone wire and throttle Mr. Stanley Brown, her cheapskate landlord.

Unfortunately, even if she could reach across the line, she'd only manage to grasp thin air, since she wasn't talking to an actual person. Instead, she was babbling, as usual, into his answering machine. "Please call me as soon as you can," she finished, trying desperately to hang on to her composure.

She slammed down the phone, picked up the

wrench and crawled beneath the sink. Shoving the pot aside, she connected the wrench to the elbow joint and tried to tighten the ring. It wouldn't budge.

She strained again, feeling her face growing red with her effort. "Whew," she said, and gave up. She simply didn't have the strength required to get it to turn.

"Hello? Anybody home?"

The deep male voice at her back door startled her. She jumped, banging her head on one of the pipes. "Who's there?" she yelled irritably, rubbing her forehead as she tried to wiggle out from beneath the cabinet.

The door opened and Caleb McMann stepped inside. In his hand he held a donut box that emitted the most delicious aromas Erica had ever smelled.

"Looks like you could use some help," he said, stating the obvious. He set the box on the table and held out a hand to help her up.

She hesitated a moment. Her first inclination was to send him packing. She didn't like his friendly smile and she'd always believed it was best to be wary of men bearing donuts.

But the rational part of her recognized she could use his help. The job required more strength than she possessed, and Caleb's forearms and bulging biceps, displayed to perfection by his white T-shirt, looked more than adequate.

She placed her hand in his and allowed him to pull

her to a standing position. "I…it's leaking and I don't have the strength to tighten it enough."

"Mind if I give it a try?" He held out his hand for the wrench she still held.

She shrugged. Why not? "Be my guest." She handed it to him and watched as he got down on the floor on his back and worked his torso into the cabinet.

It seemed impossible that his broad shoulders would fit, but he somehow managed to wedge himself beneath the pipes.

As he worked, it was also impossible for Erica not to notice the half of his body that remained in view. His abdomen was sinfully flat, his hips beneath his tight-fitting jeans were lean and his legs seemed to stretch forever. Erica's grandmother would have called him a tall drink of water…a very nicely built drink of water, Erica thought.

She suddenly became conscious that she'd pulled on her ugliest T-shirt that morning and that the jeans she wore, which had once fit her so well, now hung on her like a layer of skin she was attempting to shed. She couldn't even remember if she'd brushed her hair yet this morning. Irritation followed on the heels of these thoughts.

She didn't care what she looked like. She wasn't trying to impress anyone…especially a neighbor who apparently intended to be more neighborly than she wanted.

Hannah entered the kitchen clad in her pajamas. Peaches followed close behind. "Mr. Man!" she squealed in delight as she spied him beneath the cabinet. Peaches emitted a sharp yip.

Caleb jumped in surprise, clunking his head as Erica had done only moments before. "Ouch," he exclaimed and dropped the wrench.

"Are you all right?" Erica asked worriedly. This was all she needed, for him to get hurt and sue her. Sure, he could sue her for half her bills, she thought wryly.

"Fine…I think I got it tightened well enough." With a grunt, he squirmed out from beneath the sink, one hand rubbing his forehead.

"Did you get a boo-boo?" Hannah asked, her little face radiating sympathy.

"Only a small one," Caleb replied as he stood. He smiled at Hannah.

"I had a big boo-boo, but it's all well now," Hannah said.

"Hannah, go get dressed," Erica instructed briskly. The last thing she wanted was for Hannah to discuss her heart operation with a virtual stranger. Erica didn't believe in sharing her business with anyone.

Hannah hesitated a moment and sniffed the air. "I smell something yummy."

Caleb smiled at the little girl. "Donuts." He looked at Erica. "I thought maybe your mommy could make some coffee and we could all have a visit while we eat the donuts I brought."

"Oh, boy!" Hannah clapped her hands together. "I love donuts. They're one of the most bestest foods."

"Then go change your clothes and wash your face and hands," Erica said, fighting a renewed burst of irritation. She didn't want to make him coffee and she didn't want to "have a visit" with him over donuts.

Still, she supposed it would be boorish of her to toss him out now, and a cup of coffee seemed a small price to pay for a sink that no longer leaked.

"Please, have a seat." She gestured toward the table. "It will just take me a minute to get the coffee going."

On any other day, it would have already been made, but the first thing she'd seen upon entering the kitchen that morning had been a stream of water running out from her sink cabinet. So brewing coffee had been forgotten amid the cleanup and the futile attempt to get in touch with Stanley Brown.

Caleb eased down into one of the wooden chairs as Erica began to prepare the coffee. Peaches took her usual position, lying down beneath the table, waiting for any crumbs that might drop over the sides.

"You're going to need those sink pipes replaced fairly quickly," he said. "They're pretty old and corroded."

"I know." Erica released a deep sigh. "My landlord has been promising for months to get a plumber over here to look at them." She turned and smiled at him tightly. "He's also promised painters, the possibility of a central-air-conditioning unit and a dozen other things as well. That's Stanley Brown for you…he's big on promises but not so hot on following through. I've tried everything I can think of to get him to comply, but nothing has worked so far.''

"Take him to court,'' Caleb suggested. "Nothing like a legal petition to make a landlord comply. Sometimes even the threat itself is enough to get them motivated.''

Erica shook her head. "It's not worth the hassle. I mean, it's not as if Stanley is a slumlord. The place just needs a few odds and ends taken care of.'' She turned back to the cabinets to get out cups and saucers.

She wasn't about to tell him that this house was the best thing that had ever happened to Hannah and her. Although not in the greatest shape, the house was their first real home after a long string of apartments. Stanley, knowing the financial burden Erica struggled beneath because of medical bills and the inability to hold a full-time job, had agreed to a monthly rent that was far below market value.

"I'm back,'' Hannah announced as she reentered the kitchen. She was clad in a pair of denim shorts and a coral-colored T-shirt and her cheeks were pink from the obvious scrubbing she'd given her face.

She sat on the chair next to Caleb and eyed the red-and-white pastry box. "What kind of donuts did you bring us, Mr. Man?''

Caleb leaned toward Hannah, a gentle smile curving his lips. "I wasn't sure whether you'd like chocolate, or maybe cinnamon buns, or just plain glazed, so I brought a combination of all kinds.'' He opened the box to display the sweets.

"You may have two," Erica told her daughter as she set a cup of coffee in front of Caleb and a glass of milk before Hannah.

"Two?" Hannah echoed in dismay. She eyed the various kinds and after careful deliberation finally chose a chocolate-covered cake donut.

"Doesn't Mrs. McMann object to you bringing donuts to neighbors?" Erica asked as she joined them at the table.

"The only Mrs. McMann I know is my mother, and she hates donuts."

So he's single, Erica thought. Not that it mattered one whit to her. She wasn't sure why he was here, why he had brought donuts, but if he was looking for anything remotely resembling romance, he was definitely searching in the wrong place.

"So is there a Mr. Clemmons?" he asked.

"No." Erica offered no further information. She sipped her coffee and eyed him surreptitiously as he and Hannah launched into a conversation about the joy of donuts.

There was no denying the man's physical attractiveness. Erica guessed him to be around her age, either late twenties or early thirties. He had bold, well-defined features...a straight nose, a square chin and high cheekbones that accentuated his sensual mouth.

His face was tanned, as if he was accustomed to working outside, and when he smiled, tiny lines radiated from his eyes, starbursts of wrinkles that only added to his overall appeal.

His hair was black, lustrous and shiny, but it was his eyes that were so arresting. They reminded her of distant stars, blue with just a touch of sparkling silver.

She blushed as she realized at that moment they were focused directly at her. "The real-estate agent told me this is a pretty quiet neighborhood."

"It is," she agreed, diverting her own gaze down to her coffee cup. Now, if she could just figure out a way to divert the smell of him...a clean, masculine scent that Erica had almost forgotten existed in the world. "Mostly retired people and professionals without children. Hannah and I are sort of the odd ducks."

"Quack, quack, I'm a duck!" Hannah scooted off her chair. "Look, Mr. Man, I can walk like a duck." She proceeded to give him her best imitation of a waddling, quacking duck.

Caleb laughed again and the pleasant, utterly male sound sent a small shiver of warmth through Erica. Yet, following the rivulet of warmth came the chill of alarm.

She didn't want to find this man...or any man... appealing on any level. She didn't want or need the complications and heartbreak that relationships inevitably brought.

More than that, she refused to allow anyone to break Hannah's heart. Her daughter had been through enough with her health problems, she didn't need broken promises and dashed hopes to burden the heart that now pumped in her chest.

"Hannah, get back up here and finish eating," she

said more tersely than she intended. "Even ducks need breakfast," she added with a smile to take the sting from her sharpness.

"Okay," Hannah agreed easily and gave Erica one of the sunshine smiles that always made her heart swell with love.

"You aren't eating," Caleb observed. He shoved the pastry box toward her.

"I'm not a morning eater," she replied.

"But she eats a lot at dinnertime," Hannah quipped.

Caleb laughed, and despite Erica's embarrassment, she laughed as well. "Dinner is my favorite meal," she confessed. "My mornings are usually filled with work," she said pointedly, hoping to hurry him out. He obviously didn't get the hint. She sighed in frustration as he reached for another donut, apparently in no rush to go.

Caleb got the hint that she was ready for him to leave, but he studiously pretended to be obtuse. He wasn't prepared to go back to his empty, silent house yet.

Besides, at that moment Hannah launched into a tale about the garden she was attempting to grow in the backyard, a childish litany much like the ones Katie had often entertained him with.

As he gazed at the little girl, whose face was so animated as she told him about the carrots and radishes she'd planted, his head filled with a vision of his Katie.

Physically the two girls couldn't have been more

different, Hannah with dark hair and eyes and Katie, a blond fairy princess with bright blue eyes. Still, Caleb saw in Hannah the same enthusiasm, the same joyous embracing of life that Katie had possessed.

Had Hannah always exhibited such effervescence or had this particular quality suddenly appeared after Katie's heart had been gently placed in Hannah's chest? He needed to know this…and so much more. Time, he reminded himself. Time would answer all his questions.

"So, exactly what sort of work do you do?" he asked Erica after he and Hannah had exhausted the gardening topic.

"Bookkeeping here at home. I work for a couple of doctors and a dentist. I take care of their accounts receivable and issue monthly statements for them."

"Sounds like the best of both worlds," Caleb said. "You have a nice business, but get to do it here from your home and care take for your daughter."

She nodded. "Child care is so expensive, I wanted something that would keep me home full-time. I also edit a couple of newsletters."

"Really? What kind of newsletters?" He leaned forward, surprised to discover himself drawn to this woman, who radiated a cool composure and an aura of intense reserve.

She looked quite pretty despite her tousled hair and face devoid of makeup. She wasn't the type of striking beauty who would make men turn and stare, but she had a quiet loveliness that was very attractive.

"Different kinds," she hedged, as if unwilling to talk about herself or her work.

"Ah, that clarifies it," he said with a smile.

She blushed, the pink of her cheeks appearing to deepen the blue hue of her eyes. "There's one for mothers who work at home, another for men who drive classic cars...it's freelance work that earns me a little extra money."

"Sounds fascinating," he replied, and meant it. She was obviously a resourceful woman who was trying to make the best of her situation.

"Mr. Man?" Hannah slid off her chair and sidled up next to him. "Are you gonna build a tree house in that tree?"

"I was just thinking about that this morning," he replied. Hannah gazed at him eagerly, her big brown eyes filled with hope. "And I think that tree would look mighty magnificent holding a special house, complete with windows."

"And pink curtains?" Hannah asked, breathless with the kind of excitement only a child could maintain.

"Hannah," Erica said in protest.

"And pink curtains," he agreed, laughing as she suddenly threw her arms around his neck.

The unexpected gesture surprised him and the warmth of the hug, coupled with the sweet smell of childhood, overwhelmed him.

A shaft of pain, a breathless ache of loss engulfed

him, inundating him with wave after wave of immutable sadness.

"Hannah, run along and let Mr. McMann finish his coffee," Erica instructed her daughter.

Hannah let go of Caleb and Caleb shot up from his chair, needing to flee, to escape and be by himself. "I'd better let you get to work," he said, almost panicked with the need to remove himself before he broke down.

In three long strides he was at the back door. "I'll see you both later," he said.

"Wait...your donuts..." Erica called after him, her face registering her surprise at his abrupt departure.

"Keep them," he replied, then with a quick wave he walked out of the house.

As he hurried toward his place, even the unusually warm morning sun couldn't banish the utter bleak coldness that clutched his heart...a coldness that was as familiar as his own face in the mirror.

He felt the icy fingers of despair, the chill wind of anguish, the frigid indictment of guilt. From the moment his aunt Fanny had sent that damned doll, he'd been thrown into an arctic landscape that offered no relief.

"A big mistake." That's what his sister had told him when he'd told her of his intention to find the child who had received Katie's heart.

Once his decision had been made, it had been remarkably easy to find the information he needed. Although there were strict codes of confidentiality concerning transplant donors and recipients, Caleb remembered overhearing a nurse in the hospital telling somebody that Katie's heart was being sent to St. Louis.

An afternoon in the library reading St. Louis newspapers for the appropriate date had given Caleb his answers. On the day Katie had died, one Hannah Marie Clemmons in St. Louis had received a heart transplant. The article was a human-interest piece, indicating that a fund had been started for the little girl to help defray her medical bills.

At first, Caleb had hired a private investigator, hoping that the information the investigation yielded would be enough to satisfy his curiosity about the little girl.

The investigator had told him she lived alone with her mother and that they were struggling financially, but he'd been unable to garner the kind of information Caleb really needed. So Caleb had decided to come to St. Louis.

Now he was unsure if he'd made the right choice in coming here, in contacting them. He'd had no second doubts when he'd contacted a real-estate agent, no reservations when he'd bought the house next door to theirs. But Hannah's hug, so achingly sweet, had evoked doubts about everything.

His sister had told him over and over again to get on with his life, that his need to find Hannah was unhealthy. "Move on, Caleb," Sarah had told him.

"Keep your memories close to your heart, but allow yourself to move past them."

Everyone had advice for the grieving father, but nobody understood the force that had driven him to be here now. Even he didn't understand it. All he knew was that he had a driving need to know Hannah, to discover what, if anything, the heart retained.

Poets wrote sonnets about hearts; every emotion ever felt was expressed through the heart. How certain could scientists be that some essence of a person, even after his or her death, didn't remain and continue to live as long as the heart was alive?

If anyone could read these kinds of thoughts in his mind, he'd be whisked away to the nearest psychiatric facility, he mused ruefully.

He vaulted the chain-link fence, then sank down beneath the tree he planned to build a tree house.

Someplace in his head, he'd known that meeting Hannah would be an incredible mix of pleasure and pain. What he hadn't anticipated was the attractiveness of Hannah's mother.

A bit prickly, yes. Skittish, indeed, and yet he found himself drawn to her. He sensed sadness in her…a sadness that had its roots in something other than her daughter's health….a sadness that somehow called to the same emotion inside him.

What had happened to Hannah's father? Was Erica Clemmons a divorced woman or a widow? As the single parent of a terminally ill child, she must have gone through hell in the past several years.

He stood and walked around to the front of his house. The work crew should be arriving at any moment, ready to start the renovations that were too big for Caleb to tackle on his own.

And while the workmen did what needed to be done, Caleb would build a tree house.

He frowned as he thought of the little house he'd just left. Apparently the landlord was none too eager to provide the repairs it so desperately needed. Caleb knew without question that Erica Clemmons would eschew any help he might personally offer, but that didn't mean he couldn't arrange something with Mr. Stanley Brown to get the work done.

For Hannah, he told himself, although in truth he knew he would be doing it for Katie. And for the woman with the lovely blue eyes who seemed to be working so hard to provide for herself and her daughter.

As a pickup and a panel truck pulled up to the curb in front of his house, Caleb went out to meet the workers, his mind already racing with plans for the very special tree house he'd build for a very special little girl.

"No, Keith, I don't think it's a good idea. Maybe another time." Erica twisted the phone cord around her thumb as she spoke to her brother.

"That's what you always say," Keith protested. "It would be good for Hannah to come over and spend some time with her cousins. We never get a chance to spend any time with her.''

''Her birthday is in a couple of weeks, and I'm planning a big party. Of course you and Amy and the kids are invited. We can all visit then,'' Erica replied.

''Erica...'' Keith sighed. ''Never mind. Just let Amy know what time the party is and we'll be there.''

Erica said goodbye to her brother, then hung up the phone with a frown. Every so often Keith or Amy called and invited Hannah over to play, or to spend the night, or to go to the movies with them, and each time Erica declined on behalf of her daughter.

Erica feared that Hannah wasn't strong enough yet to spend time with Keith's three rambunctious children. Accidents happened, illnesses were passed from one child to another. It was simply too big a risk for Hannah.

She moved to the kitchen window and looked out to the backyard.

Hannah was there, digging in the little patch of her garden. She'd come in earlier, eaten an apple, then carefully picked out the seeds and run back out to plant them. Stretched out on the ground next to Hannah, Peaches watched her mistress with interest.

The evening sun was still unusually warm. Although it was only the first of June, it had already become unseasonably hot.

Beyond where Hannah was digging in the garden, Erica could see the huge tree in Caleb McMann's backyard. Yesterday Caleb had worked to build a platform in the perfect cradle of branches. Today a wall had been erected, much to Hannah's delight and Erica's consternation.

For the past two days, the air had been filled with the banging of hammers and the buzz of saws, both from inside the big house and outside where Caleb worked. She still couldn't believe he was actually building a tree house for Hannah. It just didn't make any sense.

She finished washing the last of their supper dishes, then stepped outside the back door. "Hey munchkin, how are you doing?"

"Okay," Hannah replied, waving the child-size hoe in the air. "I'm getting all the weeds away so everything will grow big and strong."

Erica nodded and eased down on the multicolored chaise longue. The evening warmth instantly produced a pleasant lethargy and she closed her eyes, able to hear the sweet music of Hannah's voice as she talked to her growing vegetables.

Erica sighed, for the moment at peace with the world. With the approach of sunset, a tiny breeze had kicked up, alleviating the intense heat of the day.

Hannah's voice became lulling white noise as sleep teased at the edges of Erica's consciousness. It had been a long day and talking to her brother always unsettled her.

Her relationship with Keith had been strained for so long. Erica sighed and gave in to the healing warmth of the sun. She didn't want to think about Keith now. She didn't want to think about anything.

"Hey, neighbor."

The familiar deep male voice jarred her out of her drowsy state. She kept her eyes firmly closed, tension instantly tightening relaxed muscles. Maybe if she pretended to be asleep, he'd go away.

"Mommy, look who came to visit." With little fingers, Hannah pried open one of Erica's eyelids. "See, Mr. Man is here."

Caleb McMann, her own personal version of Mr. Rogers in the neighborhood, stood holding a tray with three tall glasses of what appeared to be pink lemonade.

However, Mr. Rogers would never appear shirtless, nor would he look as good as Caleb did at the moment. Caleb, with his expanse of tanned, muscled chest and a smattering of dark chest hair, banished all sleepiness, all pretense of relaxation.

This man is dangerous, a tiny voice whispered in the back of her head. He was temptation to all the things Erica had put behind her, all the emotions she'd sworn she'd never feel again. He was a man to be avoided at all costs, a man who could make her remember things better left forgotten.

What was he doing here? Why did he seem so intent on being friendly with her? What was he doing popping in and out of her house, fixing sinks, building tree houses, bearing donuts, then lemonade? What did he want from her?

She sat up, deciding it was definitely time to explain to Mr. Rogers in no uncertain terms that she wanted him out of her neighborhood.

Chapter 3

"Mr. McMann," Erica began as she sat up in her chair. She was acutely conscious of the fact that her denim cutoffs were almost indecently short and her T-shirt was far too tight. She hadn't exactly been expecting company.

"Please...make it Caleb." He grinned boyishly as he set the tray of refreshments on the nearby picnic table, then carried one of the glasses back to where she was seated. "It's so warm this evening that lemonade seemed to be in order."

Reluctantly Erica took the glass from him.

"I love lemonade," Hannah said, reaching for the smallest of the glasses left on the tray.

Erica looked at her daughter in surprise. Hannah had never professed to loving lemonade before. It seemed

Caleb McMann was a hit with at least one of the Clemmons ladies.

She frowned, watching as Caleb grabbed the last glass and sat down on the picnic bench. Hannah perched beside him and smiled up at him.

Erica had a feeling her daughter didn't love lemonade as much as she was growing fond of Mr. Caleb McMann. *Daddy eyes,* that's what Hannah had said about the man the first day she'd met him.

Daddy eyes, indeed! Erica needed to nip this in the bud somehow. The last thing she wanted was for her daughter to get any ideas about Caleb having any special place in their lives. She intended to protect her daughter from any hurt.

"People in this neighborhood don't usually do much casual socializing," Erica said, her voice cool and holding a slight note of censure.

Caleb shrugged and leaned over to scratch Peaches behind her ears. "I guess that makes me one of three odd ducks in town." He grinned at Hannah and winked. "Quack," he said.

Hannah giggled and Erica sighed, realizing her attempt to make a point had drifted away with the warm evening breeze.

"Where I come from, neighbors are neighborly," he said. "That's the way it should be in the world."

"And where are you from Mr., uh, Caleb?" Erica asked.

"Originally, a little tiny town in Illinois. More recently, Chicago."

"I can't imagine Chicago being so very different from St. Louis," she said dryly.

"True," he agreed. "But both Chicago and St. Louis are very different from Shady Bluff, Illinois. In that little town folks knew how to be friendly."

Erica had never heard of Shady Bluff, Illinois. "And what brings you to St. Louis?"

He paused a moment to take a sip of his drink. "Sort of a working vacation."

The answer was vague and Erica eyed him curiously. "A working vacation?"

"Yeah, you know...you go on vacation but you accomplish a little work at the same time." He smiled at her, but the smile did nothing to alleviate the whisper of distrust that swept through Erica. His answer hadn't really been an answer at all.

Before she had a chance to ask him more questions, he turned and smiled at Hannah.

"So, little Miss Muffet who sat on a tuffet. How does your garden grow?"

Hannah giggled once again. "That's not right. It's Mary, Mary, quite contrary. And it grows just fine. Wanna see?"

"Sure," he agreed. He set his drink down and stood as Hannah jumped up and eagerly danced toward her garden. He smiled at Erica. "I'll be right back."

"Don't hurry on my account," she muttered, watching as he walked with long strides behind Hannah.

It irritated her that he looked just as good going as he did coming. His broad, bare back gleamed a honeyed brown and muscles rippled beneath the bronzed skin. A wave of heat swept through her, heat that had nothing to do with the day's temperature.

Despite her desire to the contrary, curiosity niggled at her. She wondered what exactly he did for a living, why he'd left Chicago for St. Louis. What exactly was "a working vacation"? Sounded like a sinful indulgence to her.

It was obvious from the work going on at his house that money didn't seem to be a problem for him. During the several days since he'd moved in, she hadn't seen him leave the house for any extended period of time. So, what kind of work did he do?

The questions fluttered through her mind. What had brought him to St. Louis? And more importantly, what had brought him to the house next door to theirs? He appeared to have lots of money yet no visible means of support. Again an edge of distrust sliced through her. Who was Caleb McMann and why did he seem to be going out of his way to spend time with her and Hannah?

She shoved the question from her mind.

She didn't care to know about his personal life. Sharing personal information bred familiarity, and familiarity was definitely what Erica intended to avoid at all costs.

She sipped the cool drink and eyed Caleb, who was now crouched beside Hannah as the little girl pointed out the vegetables that had begun to peek out of the earth.

He appeared to be listening intently to whatever Hannah was telling him. The little girl seemed to have his complete, undivided attention.

Okay, Erica mentally conceded. So the man made delicious lemonade, looked sinfully terrific without his shirt, and showed an inordinate amount of patience with small children. That didn't mean she was interested. Curious, yes. Interested, no.

She tensed as Caleb and Hannah stood, then Caleb walked back to where she sat. "That's some little garden she's got growing," Caleb exclaimed as he once again sat down on the picnic bench.

Erica nodded. "She's been very good at weeding and watering every evening. She's always liked working outside, even when she was very small."

Erica relaxed as memories swept through her. Even when Hannah was at her sickest, the thing she'd minded most wasn't the shots or the medicines but being cooped up inside. "She's more than a little bit of a tomboy."

"Nothing wrong with that," Caleb replied. He focused intently on her. "What about you? Are you a tomboy? In your spare time do you like to work outside and participate in sports, or do you prefer candle-lit dinners and going to the theater?"

"I have very little free time and what little I do have, I spend with my daughter." Sherry would have called Erica's tone her ice-maiden voice, and Erica offered him a small smile to temper it.

"That's commendable," he said, apparently not put

off by her momentary burst of attitude. "But doesn't it also result in a rather lonely kind of life?"

She felt the blush that warmed her cheeks. "I like being alone. I tried it the other way—the happily-ever-after, soul-mates-forever route—and discovered it wasn't exactly what the hype promised." She shut her mouth with an audible click of her teeth, irritated that she'd said more than she'd intended.

"Divorced, huh?"

She nodded. "What about you?"

"Widower." He said the word softly, and in his silvery gaze Erica saw the dark shadows of loss, like an eclipse momentarily stealing away the light.

"I've gardened enough," Hannah exclaimed as she rejoined them. She sat down next to Caleb and picked up her drink. She drank deeply, then grinned at them both. "I think I got all the weeds. My best friend says I should plant some flowers with the vegetables. Pretty pink and red flowers."

"Your best friend?" Erica looked at her daughter curiously.

Hannah nodded. "My dream friend." Hannah took another sip of her lemonade, then continued. "I don't know her name, but sometimes she comes in my dreams and we have fun and play together."

A dream friend. Erica smiled at her daughter. "I used to have a dream friend when I was little, only mine was a big, fat, furry teddy bear."

"And mine was a bald-headed cowboy named Curly," Caleb said.

For a brief moment Erica felt the unity that suddenly joined the three of them, a fellowship created by the crazy sharing of imaginary friends.

"My friend plays hopscotch and jumps rope with me," Hannah said.

"Teddy used to have tea parties with me," Erica returned.

"Cowboy Curly used to let me chew tobacco."

Both Erica and Hannah made sounds of disgust as Caleb laughed. "Trust me…as I recall, dream chewing tobacco tasted like bubble gum."

"Speaking of dreams…." Erica looked at Hannah. "I'm dreaming of a little girl in her pajamas and ready for bed."

Hannah sighed. "I think she's talking about me," she said to Caleb.

He laughed again. "I think you're right."

Hannah slid off the bench and looked beseechingly at Erica. "Maybe you dreamed about a little girl putting on her pajamas and going to bed later tonight?" she asked hopefully.

Erica shook her head. "Nope. Hurry along now, it's getting late."

Hannah sighed once again, then touched the top of Peaches' head. "Come on, Peaches. We gotta go get ready for bed."

"And make sure you wash your face and hands and brush your teeth," Erica called after her. "When you're finished, come get me and I'll tuck you in."

Hannah and Peaches disappeared into the house and

for a moment the only sound was the noise of nocturnal insects coming awake and filling the air with their songs.

Dusk painted the western sky in vivid shades of plum and although Erica knew she should get up, go inside and encourage Caleb McMann to go home, she didn't move.

"Dusk has always been my favorite time of day," she said. She remembered the days of Hannah's illness. Each evening as twilight approached, she'd take a moment to say a prayer of thanks for the fact that they'd gotten through another day together.

"It is nice," Caleb agreed. He took a sip of his lemonade, then looked in the direction of his backyard. "In another week or two we can all watch the sunset from the tree house."

Erica frowned. "You shouldn't be building a tree house just because Hannah wanted one."

He looked at her in mock innocence. "But I've always wanted a tree house," he protested.

She eyed him with a dry smile. "With real windows?"

He nodded soberly, although his eyes twinkled with merriment. "And pink curtains. It's been a long, unrealized dream of mine."

Erica laughed and shook her head ruefully. It still didn't make sense to her. But if Caleb had his heart set on building Hannah a tree house who was she to put up a fight?

Besides, the man really did have a charming appeal.

And just because he was drop-dead handsome and charismatic, that didn't mean he had to be anything more to her than a pleasant neighbor, she told herself.

"So, what sort of work do you do?" she asked curiously.

"I own a construction company."

"You build houses?" she asked.

He shook his head. "Commercial. Shopping malls and office buildings, that sort of thing."

"You mentioned a working vacation. Is your company building here in St. Louis?"

"No." He sighed and raked a hand through his thick hair. "I worked pretty hard over the last year and I suddenly realized I'd gotten far afield from what I truly loved doing...working with my hands." He pointed toward his place. "I decided to find a handyman special and get back to some basic carpentry."

"Why here? In St. Louis?"

He shrugged. "Why not?"

Erica frowned. It didn't make sense. "Had you visited here before?"

He studied her for a moment, then quickly nodded. "Yeah...uh...when I was younger, my family went on vacations here in St. Louis and so when I decided to take a little time off, this seemed to be the place to come to."

"You have family back in Chicago?"

"No. They're all back in Shady Bluff. My sister Sarah teaches fifth grade and my brother John is the sheriff."

"Are you close to them?" It irritated her, the slight yearning she heard in her own voice.

"John and I are fairly close, but there are days I'd swear I've got ten sisters. She has enough maternal instinct to parent forty children."

"Sounds nice, though," Erica said.

"All done," Hannah announced as she came out the back door, followed closely by the apricot poodle.

"Hands," Erica said. Hannah held up her hands for inspection. "Good. And your face looks all clean, too."

Hannah nodded. "I scrubbed real good."

"Then why don't you tell Mr. McMann good-night and I'll tuck you in," Erica said.

"I want Mr. Man to tuck me in."

Tension immediately wafted from Caleb.

"Hannah...we don't want to bother..."

"It's no bother," Caleb said, interrupting Erica's protest as he stood. "I'd be delighted to tuck in the lovely Miss Hannah."

Hannah giggled, her miniature features radiating hero worship as she gazed at Caleb. She held out her hand for him to grasp and together man and child headed for the back door; Erica followed just behind.

She tried not to feel any embarrassment as they walked through the living room, where her bedding from the night before was still on the sofa. She didn't owe anyone any explanations for where she slept in her own home, she told herself firmly.

Hannah had the largest of the two bedrooms and

Erica was pleased that the small window-unit air-conditioner made the room comfortable. The room was like a burst of sunshine. Yellow curtains hung at the window and a matching spread covered the bed. Lined up against one wall a variety of stuffed animals watched with button eyes as Caleb pulled down the bedspread.

Erica stopped in the doorway and motioned Peaches to her doggy bed in the corner.

"First you have to say good-night to Harry," Hannah explained as she crawled into bed and beneath the sheet.

"Harry?"

"Harry the hamster," Erica said, and gestured to the cage on the dresser.

"Ah." Caleb walked over to the dresser and peered into the cage. "Good evening, Harry. You're a fine-looking fellow."

"He likes to run on his wheel at night," Hannah said.

Caleb nodded. "Yes, I've heard only the smartest hamsters do that." He walked back to the side of the bed and sat down on the edge of the mattress. "Okay...arms in or out?" he asked.

"Out." Hannah placed her arms on top of the sheet.

"Do you usually get a bedtime story?" Caleb asked.

"No, but if you know a good one you could tell it to me."

"Hannah..." Erica said with a warning.

"No bedtime story," Hannah replied with a sigh.

"Good, because I'd have had to make one up," Caleb replied.

Erica smiled, wondering what kind of story Caleb McMann would have produced. She imagined he'd be quite creative, and equally amusing.

"Good night, Hannah." He stood and leaned over and kissed her on the forehead.

"'Night, Mr. Man. Good night, Mommy," Hannah replied, her eyes already drifting closed.

Caleb joined Erica in the doorway. He threaded his fingers through his hair and for just a moment Erica thought his hand trembled. His eyes appeared darker than usual as he looked back at Hannah. "Is she asleep already?"

Erica nodded. "She's always done that. She plays hard and sleeps hard. When sleep hits, it's like a switch has turned her off. Bedtime has never really been a problem."

Suddenly Erica was aware of how close Caleb stood to her. She was aware of a provocative warmth that smelled of virile male. His nearness seemed to be drawing in all the oxygen, making breathing more difficult for her.

For a moment, Erica had an insane desire to lean against him and feel his arms wrap around her and hold her close.

What a pleasure it would be to feel for just a moment the support of another. She stepped out of the doorway and away from him. "Thank you for tucking her in,'' she said briskly as they entered the living room.

''No problem. She's a terrific kid.''

To her dismay, he shoved aside the blue-flowered sheet on the sofa and sat down, apparently in no hurry to leave. To her bigger dismay was the knowledge that she wasn't in any hurry for him to leave, either.

Caleb had been doing very well with Hannah. He'd enjoyed seeing her little garden, listening to her childish tales and he hadn't once experienced the abiding ache of loss.

And then she'd asked him to tuck her in. The simple act of putting her to bed and kissing her forehead had brought forth memories of a hundred different nights when he'd tucked Katie in. Her warm little arms encircling his neck, her sleepy breath against his throat…those moments before sleep had been precious to both father and daughter.

For just a moment, he'd wanted to run from Hannah's room, indulge the tears that burned hot at his eyes, give in to the familiar clutches of crippling grief.

But, he hadn't. And the need to escape had passed. Maybe he was getting stronger. He desperately hoped so. Katie wouldn't have wanted him destroyed by grief. She'd always thought he was big and strong, and he desperately wanted to be strong.

Caleb wasn't sure what he was doing now, lingering here. Hannah was in bed. There was really no reason for him to remain, and yet he was reluctant to leave.

He wasn't ready to return to the big house with its overwhelming quiet.

Besides, in the past hour or so he'd felt a thawing in Erica, a lessening of the reserve that surrounded her like an impenetrable barrier. He found himself more and more drawn to the woman beneath the veneer.

He'd believed he'd never be interested in another woman again after Judith had passed away. And for the past six years since her death there had been no other female in his life other than his daughter.

"Would you like some coffee?" she asked.

"Sure, if it isn't too much trouble." He was pleased by the offer, a further indication that she was thawing out a bit.

"No trouble." Her face flushed slightly as she quickly grabbed up the sheet and bed pillow. "Sorry...I wasn't expecting company."

"Hey, don't apologize." He gestured to the ceiling fan that was stirring the warm air in the room. "I'm sure it's cooler in here with the fan."

She nodded, placed the bedding on a nearby chair, then disappeared into the kitchen.

Caleb looked around the room with interest. He'd always believed you could tell a lot about a person by the things they surrounded themselves with in their home.

Erica was obviously a woman who shunned clutter. There were no knickknacks, no collectibles gathering dust on the end tables or in the built-in bookcase. He wanted to believe that this was because she was a woman who valued intangibles rather than physical possessions.

The bookcase held several thick medical tomes, framed pictures of Hannah and a container of computer disks. It was obvious Hannah was Erica's world. Caleb knew how easy it was to build a life around a child. He'd done the same thing with Katie after Judith's death.

The sofa and matching chairs were a dark beige, with accent stripes in dark green and burgundy. Nice, although a relatively inexpensive brand, he noted. He remembered the investigator's report, of overwhelming medical bills and a hand-to-mouth existence for them.

"Here we are," Erica said as she reentered the room carrying a tray laden with coffee mugs. "You take yours black, right?"

"Right." He jumped up and took the tray from her and sat it down on the table in front of the sofa. He grabbed a cup and held it out to her. As she took it from him, their fingers brushed, and he thought he felt a slight tremor in hers. Maybe she wasn't quite as immune to him as she would have him think.

The heart he'd thought dead and buried lurched inside him and suddenly began to pump in an erratic rhythm. He grabbed the remaining coffee mug from the tray and sank back down on the sofa as she sat in a chair facing him. His attraction to her confused him.

"How's the work coming on your house?" she asked.

"Fine…although the workmen have really just barely scratched the surface. The house was in pretty bad shape." He tried not to notice the length of her tanned legs, the thrust of her breasts against the snug, pale blue T-shirt she wore.

"It's been empty for as long as Hannah and I have lived here."

"And how long is that?"

"Almost a year.

"And before here?"

She took a sip of her coffee, then replied. "Several apartments around town."

"Are you from the St. Louis area originally?" Caleb felt as if they were drowning in inane chatter. What he really wanted to know was if she tasted as good as she smelled, if her eyes would darken to midnight blue when he kissed her.

He had no idea where these sort of thoughts were coming from.

"Born and raised here," she replied.

"You have family?" He remembered the momentary wistfulness he'd heard in her tone when she'd asked him about his family.

"My father left our family when I was twelve and I haven't seen or heard from him since. My mother passed away before Hannah was born. I have a brother here in town, but we aren't really close."

"That's too bad. Nothing better than family to help get you through the hard times."

She tilted her head, her long curtain of hair falling

to one side. "It must have been tough, losing your wife. Was it an accident?" she asked tentatively, as if afraid of intruding on his privacy.

"No. Judith had cancer. She was ill for quite some time before finally succumbing to the disease." Although Caleb felt a sense of sadness, he'd long ago grieved for the spouse he had lost. Now, it was like the ache of a dear friend's absence.

"Long-term illnesses are so difficult," Erica said. Her eyes peered at him intently, as if not only looking at him, but into him. "Didn't you ever think of leaving her? Getting away from the pain?"

He looked at her in surprise. "It never crossed my mind. I wanted to be with her...I needed to be with her...to comfort her until she breathed her last breath and was no longer with me on this earth."

Sudden tears shimmered in her eyes, making him wonder what experiences she'd had with her ex-husband and with Hannah's illness. But he couldn't very well ask her, since she didn't know he knew about Hannah's heart problems. In any case, the tears were gone with a blink of her eyes.

"She was a very lucky woman," she said softly.

He smiled and shook his head. "No, I was a very lucky man. We had three wonderful years together before she got sick. And even the bad times had moments of joy." He consciously willed away the memory of the promise he'd made to Judith on her deathbed...the promise he hadn't been able to keep.

He cleared his throat. "We're getting rather maudlin here."

"Yes, we are. I'm sorry." She smiled apologetically. Silence fell between them, an uncomfortable silence as they each strained for something to say.

"So, when..." she began.

"I guess..." he said at the same time. They laughed self-consciously. "You first," he prompted.

"I was just going to ask how long it takes to build a tree house."

"It should be finished up in a week or so... depending on the weather."

"According to the weather forecast, that shouldn't be a problem. I heard it's supposed to stay unseasonably hot and humid." She frowned, as if dreading the days to come.

"I guess this is what they refer to as the dog days of summer."

She laughed. "Not hardly. If you think this is bad...wait until August. *That's* when we experience the dog days. It gets so thick, so sweltering it's difficult to draw breath." She frowned, and he guessed she was imagining this little house cooking in the August heat without the pleasure of air-conditioning.

I'll probably be gone by August, Caleb thought. His plan had always been to stay in St. Louis a couple of weeks...perhaps a month, make sure that all was well with Hannah Clemmons, then he'd return to his penthouse apartment in Chicago.

"Now, what were you going to say?" she asked.

He finished his coffee with a quick swallow, then set the cup back on the tray. "I was going to say that I guess it's time for me to head back home." He stood, reluctant to leave, confused by his desire to remain, to learn more about Erica.

Erica walked him to the back door and together they stepped out into the night shadows that had fallen. "Thanks for the coffee," he said.

She smiled up at him. "Thanks for the lemonade," she returned.

He wanted to kiss her. All he'd have to do was take a single step forward and dip his head and he could claim her lips with his own. His desire had nothing to do with his need to know Hannah. It was all about Erica.

He took the step forward, his desire swelling when she didn't retreat. Instead, she tilted her head slightly back, as if anticipating...and welcoming his kiss.

What are you doing, McMann? a little voice whispered inside his head. Was it possible that this was really about Hannah? Was it possible he needed so badly for just a little while to be a part of Hannah's life that he was manufacturing some sort of desire for Hannah's mother?

Truthfully, he wasn't sure. If so, then kissing Erica wasn't fair to her and it wasn't fair to him.

He took a step backward and instead of kissing her, he reached up and lightly touched her cheek with the tip of his fingers. "Good night, Erica."

"'Night, Caleb."

He turned and hurried home. When he reached the fence, he hopped over it, then went into the house and directly to the phone.

On the pad next to the phone was a number and he quickly punched it in.

It wasn't fair to kiss Erica when he didn't know for sure what motivated him. But that didn't mean he couldn't do something to make things easier on both her and Hannah.

"Hello?" A deep, male voice answered the phone at the other end of the line.

"Mr. Brown? Stanley Brown? You don't know me, but I have a proposition for you," Caleb began.

Chapter 4

"Cheapskate Stanley is paying for a central-air unit?" Sherry stared at Erica in utter amazement. "Is he on heavy medication? Has he had a lobotomy?"

Erica laughed. "I don't know what got into him, but yesterday the men from Walters Furnace and Air Conditioning showed up to see what they needed to do to install a complete unit."

The two women, along with Hannah, sat in a booth in Reggie's Restaurant, a small neighborhood establishment that offered reasonable prices and an atmosphere conducive to relaxed conversation.

"All I know," Erica continued, "is that I'm not about to look a gift horse in the mouth." She leaned back against the cracked blue leather seat. "It will be glorious to have a house that's cool throughout…to get to sleep in my own bed instead of on the sofa."

"I still don't get it." Sherry popped a French fry into her mouth. "Stanley has bucked and kicked at every dollar you've asked him to spend on repairs on that house and now suddenly he's popping for an entire air-conditioning unit."

"Mr. Man is building me a tree house," Hannah told Sherry.

"Mr. Man?" Sherry looked first at Hannah, then at Erica. "Who is Mr. Man?"

"Caleb McMann. He bought the big house next door. He's building a big tree house for Hannah in the tree in his backyard." Erica focused her gaze down on her plate, her cheeks warming slightly at the thought of Caleb.

"Really." Sherry drew the word into three long syllables. Erica looked up to see her friend's blond eyebrows raised in speculation. "Soooo…single or married? Prince or a toad?"

"Single. And not a prince or a toad. Just a man," Erica replied. She wished Hannah had never brought up the topic of Caleb McMann. Now Sherry would chew on it like a dog with a rawhide bone.

"I like him," Hannah exclaimed. "He has daddy eyes."

Sherry's brows nearly shot off the top of her forehead. "Indeed? Daddy eyes, huh? And what exactly are 'daddy eyes'?"

Hannah grinned, delighted at having Sherry's undivided attention. "Nice, with little blue sparkles.

They look just like a daddy's eyes are supposed to look.''

Erica sighed and once again gazed at what remained of her hamburger, ignoring Sherry's obvious amusement. She picked up a fry. "He's just a neighbor," she repeated with a slight edge of irritation.

"He brung us donuts."

"Brought, doll face," Sherry corrected Hannah. "He brought you donuts?"

"Don't make a big deal out of this, Sherry." Erica pointed the fry at her friend like a gun. "Trust me, it's not a big deal."

For the last five days Erica had gone out of her way to make sure that Caleb's friendliness didn't *become* a big deal. She'd stayed in the house, remained unavailable for any more friendly chatter.

The weathermen had been wrong in their forecast, and for the past five days rain had darkened the skies. The wet weather had provided a perfect reason to keep Hannah playing inside in the cool of her room instead of in the backyard.

No way did she intend to be drawn into any kind of a relationship with Caleb McMann, or any member of the male species.

"So tell me what you're working on," she asked Sherry. "What kind of story is Lois Lane trying to crack open?"

Sherry grinned at her knowingly. "Not particularly smooth. But I get the hint and will now change the subject." She popped another fry. "Corruption in the lunch room at Winthrop High School. There is supposed to be a gang stealing lunch money from students.''

"Sounds interesting," Erica said, trying desperately to keep her thoughts off of her handsome new neighbor.

Sherry leaned forward. "We have an opening at the paper for another reporter. Why don't you apply for it?"

"I can't do that," Erica replied.

"Why not?" Sherry demanded. "Erica, things are going well now." She reached over and tousled Hannah's hair. "This little doll face is healthier than she's ever been in her life. You know Keith and Amy would baby-sit whenever you needed them to. Isn't it time for you to get on with your own life?"

"Does somebody pay you to meddle?" Erica asked.

Sherry leaned forward once again and touched Erica's hand. "Nobody has to pay me. I meddle because I care. You're young and beautiful and bright, and you're wasting so many gifts."

"We'll discuss this later, Sherry." Erica shot her a meaningful look, then gazed at Hannah, who apparently sensed the tension between the two grown-ups. A little frown danced across the center of her forehead.

"Are you and Sherry mad, Mommy?"

"No, sweetie." Erica grabbed Sherry's hand and gave it a quick squeeze. "It's all right for friends to disagree and still be friends."

Hannah nodded. "Sometimes my dream friend and

me disagree.'' Hannah wrinkled her nose in distaste. ''My dream friend likes to play with dolls and I don't.''

''Dream friend?'' Sherry looked at Erica.

''You know...an imaginary friend,'' Erica explained.

''Mr. Man used to have a 'maginary friend called Curly the Cowboy,'' Hannah explained, then giggled. ''And he let Mr. Man chew tobacco.''

''This Mr. Man sounds utterly fascinating,'' Sherry said.

''I'll tell you what I find fascinating,'' Erica replied. ''That the conversation is being dominated with talk of a man who is nothing but a neighbor. Can we please change the subject?''

Sherry gazed intently at Erica, then shrugged. ''Okay. Have I told you the latest gossip at the paper?''

As Sherry launched into an entertaining monologue of office politics, Erica leaned back against the booth and tried to relax, tried to shove away thoughts of Caleb McMann.

Thoughts of the handsome man had been disturbing her ever since the last time they'd talked. When he'd told her about his wife's illness, her heart had opened just a touch to him.

Here was a man who'd faced enormous adversity and he hadn't run away, he hadn't turned his back. Instead, he'd faced the pain and the heartache of loss.

Just before he left, as they'd lingered for a moment

at her door, she'd had the distinct impression that he wanted to kiss her. She'd seen the kiss in his eyes and it horrified her that for just a moment, she'd wanted to feel the warmth of his mouth against hers.

However, before any contact had occurred, he'd backed away, making her wonder if she'd only imagined that kiss in his eyes.

Crazy...she didn't even know the man at all. She didn't want or need another man in her life. She had decided long ago that she would never again allow herself to be vulnerable, allow a man to hurt her...or hurt Hannah. They were fine all by themselves. A man had no place in their lives.

So, why was she wondering about Caleb's kiss? Crazy.

"So, when are they actually going to start installing the air-conditioning unit?" Sherry asked, making Erica realize she'd exhausted the topic of office gossip and had moved on.

"Tomorrow. From what the workmen told me, it's going to be a fairly big job. New ductwork is going to have to be put in and some of the old pulled out."

Sherry wrinkled her nose. "Sounds like a mess."

"Who cares about the mess? We'll be cool as cucumbers this summer."

Hannah giggled. "Cool as cucumbers. Pretty as peas."

"Soothing as squash," a deep male voice added.

"Mr. Man!" Hannah exclaimed in delight as Caleb appeared next to their booth.

"Hi, pumpkin." He tapped the tip of Hannah's nose, then smiled at Erica and Sherry.

Warmth flooded through Erica at the brilliance of his smile. Drat the man anyway, she thought as she felt the heat rise to her cheeks.

"Hi. Sherry Burnett. And you must be Caleb McMann. I've just been hearing so much about you," Sherry said, somehow successfully avoiding the kick Erica sent her beneath the table.

"I told her you're building me a tree house," Hannah said.

"I am and now that the sun is shining once again, the roof is going on one day this week."

"Oh, goody!" Hannah exclaimed.

"Please…join us." Sherry scooted over to allow him to sit next to her. She studiously ignored the glare Erica sent in her direction.

"I'll sit for just a minute. I'm meeting a contractor for lunch, but I don't see him here yet." He smiled at Erica. "How are you? The rain sort of made us all prisoners in our houses," Caleb said.

She nodded. "I've been busy."

He smiled, that damnable grin that made his eyes twinkle. "You know what they say about all work and no play."

"Yeah…it makes a person productive," she retorted, then flushed slightly, knowing she was being unusually surly.

"On the contrary…it makes a person cranky," Sherry said, earning her another pointed frown from

Erica. "Don't mind her," Sherry said to Caleb. "I understand you bought the house next to Erica's."

As Caleb and Sherry talked about the renovations Caleb was doing, Erica found herself studying the man who had been occupying too much of her thoughts.

This afternoon he looked far too attractive in a short-sleeved blue pinstripe shirt, the silvery blue stripes perfectly matching his eyes. The short sleeves displayed shapely biceps and tanned flesh. His dark hair was slightly tousled, several strands boyishly errant across his forehead.

She suddenly realized his gaze was on her. He was watching her watching him. She blushed again, irritated with him, and even more irritated with herself.

She toyed with her paper napkin, then straightened the silverware next to her plate, still acutely conscious of his lingering gaze.

"Mommy. I have to go to the bathroom," Hannah whispered.

"Okay, honey. I'll take you." Erica excused herself and her daughter, wanting to kiss Hannah soundly for her perfectly timed nature call.

In the bathroom, she splashed her face with cool water, wondering why every time Caleb McMann was around, the room temperature seemed to climb to uncomfortable heights.

It felt remarkably like sexual attraction. But it couldn't be, because Erica refused to accept that kind of chemistry in her life. Sexual attraction inevitably led to sex, which led to hope and promises that eventually would be shattered and broken. She'd learned that the hard way.

However, Erica also knew that no matter how she denied it, she was attracted to Caleb McMann, and that made him the enemy.

"We were just talking about movies," Sherry said to Erica as she and Hannah returned to the booth. "Did you know that the Uptowner is playing classics all week?"

"Really?" Sherry knew how much Erica loved the old classics.

"And tonight they're playing one of your favorites," Sherry continued, *"It Happened One Night."*

Erica smiled as she thought of the Clark Gable, Claudette Colbert romantic comedy. "One of the best movies ever made, as far as I'm concerned."

"My sentiments exactly," Caleb agreed.

"So, if you both love that movie and it's playing tonight, why don't the two of you go together to see it?" Sherry smiled, looking immensely pleased with herself. "I'll be glad to baby-sit Hannah."

"Yeah, go with Mr. Man, Mommy. I want Sherry to baby-sit me!" Hannah declared, instantly becoming an unwitting accomplice in Sherry's evil matchmaking scheme.

Caleb's gaze once again sought Erica's, those bewitching eyes of his soft and sexy. "I'm free this evening. I'd love to take you to the movies."

"And Hannah and I will spend the evening finger painting and eating junk food," Sherry added.

"Oh yes, Mommy. I love finger painting and I love junk food," Hannah replied like a tiny parrot.

Erica frowned at Sherry. She'd done this on purpose, manipulated her daughter with bribery and maneuvered Erica into a corner where to refuse would not only make her look churlish, but would disappoint Hannah as well.

She would kill Sherry later, she decided. Late at night...in the dark...when nobody would know.

"All right, but we'll go dutch," she said, hoping he understood that she didn't consider the outing anything like a real date.

He nodded, amusement flickering in his eyes. "That's fine. Whatever makes you comfortable."

It would make her comfortable if his eyes didn't shine quite so brightly, if his shoulders weren't so wonderfully broad. And she'd be really comfortable if she could pull on an old pair of sweats and watch the movie alone in her living room while Hannah played in her room.

"I think the movie starts at eight. Why don't I pick you up at seven-thirty?"

"Great!" Sherry chimed in. "She'll be ready."

"Then I'll just leave you three ladies to finish up your lunch." With a nod, he turned and left them, heading for a table in the front of the restaurant where a white-haired man was already seated.

"Whew...that's some neighbor," Sherry said when he'd gone.

"I'm going to kill you," Erica muttered in an undertone.

Sherry laughed. "Mellow out. It will be good for you."

"I can't believe you did that."

"Did what?" Sherry held out her hands in mock innocence. "I didn't do anything."

"You know perfectly well what you did, and I'm going to make you pay."

"Mommy, are you and Sherry disagreeing again?" Hannah asked.

"Yes, honey. We are," Erica replied.

Hannah smiled and reached for her mother's hand, then for Sherry's. Putting the hands together, she beamed at them both. "Friends can disagree and still be friends," she said proudly.

Erica looked at her daughter, then looked at her best friend, then laughed and shook her head ruefully. "You win this round, my friend. But if you persist in your meddling, I'm going to resort to vile methods to make you stop."

Sherry grinned. "I'll worry about that later. Right now I'm too busy worrying about finger painting with an almost-six-year-old."

They finished their meal, then Sherry insisted she take Hannah home. "There's no point in bringing her over later. I'm off for the rest of the day and this will give you all afternoon to get ready for your big date."

"It isn't a *date*," Erica corrected heatedly. "It's two neighbors who just happen to be going to the same place and sharing transportation. And really, I don't mind bringing Hannah by later." A stab of panic tightened Erica's chest. Hannah had never been away from her before for any real length of time. What if something went wrong?

Sherry smiled and patted Erica's arm as if reading her mind. "Hannah will be fine, Erica."

"Yeah, Mommy, I'll be fine," Hannah exclaimed, her cheeks pink with the excitement of a new adventure. "I want to go with Sherry."

Erica nodded, emotion clogging the back of her throat as she saw how eager her daughter was. She's growing up, Erica thought with a sharp pang. It's natural that she would look forward to a little independence, a little time away from Mom.

Sherry stood. "Come on, squirt. Let's go to my place and see what fun we can find."

As Sherry and Hannah left the restaurant, Erica fought back a renewed surge of panic.

Somehow in the past few minutes things had spun completely out of her control. Not only was Hannah going to spend an entire evening away from her, but she was supposed to spend the evening in the company of Caleb McMann. She wasn't sure which was more frightening.

"Katie, you know you're supposed to buckle up," Caleb said to his daughter in the back seat of the car as he turned onto the highway. He looked at his wristwatch and frowned.

They were running late. Mrs. Henderson, his house-keeper, was down with the flu, leaving Caleb to get his daughter ready for school while he also prepared for a day of meetings. He stepped harder on the gas and once again shot a glance in his rearview mirror.

"Katie Rose...if I have to stop this car and buckle you up..." he warned.

She stood and leaned over the front seat with a giggle. "If you stop the car, I'll just give you a big kiss, Daddy Doodle."

Caleb had no opportunity to reply. He had a single, clear picture of the truck that crossed into his lane. A bright red semi with a shiny silver grill...how odd that the driver didn't appear to see his car.

Before the imminent danger could register in his mind, there was an incredible cacophony of sound—screeching metal, shattering glass, crushing pain in his chest, the inability to breath...then nothing.

Caleb awoke, gasping for breath, covered with perspiration and crying his daughter's name over and over again.

He sat up, surprised to find himself on the sofa, surprised that he had been having a nightmare. It had felt so real. The truck...Katie Rose...that horrifying moment when he knew a crash was imminent.

He swiped his face with trembling hands, then reached for the glass of iced tea on the coffee table. The ice cubes had melted, but he hoped the sweet tea would take away the bitter taste of agony.

He drank deeply of the lukewarm liquid, then checked his watch. Six-thirty. He had an hour before it was time to pick up Erica.

He'd met with the contractor whose men were working on the house just after one. The meeting had lasted until after two, then Caleb had come home, worked a little bit, then decided to stretch out for a short nap.

For months, he hadn't been sleeping well at night. Sleep, instead of bringing rest, brought dreams... dreams of his daughter, haunting nightmares retelling the past, night after night evoking in him the recurrent struggle to change the events that had brought him to this place in time.

This was the first time those dreams had invaded a nap. He stood and padded into the kitchen, fighting off a wave of depression. Would he ever again enjoy sweet slumber unbroken by dreams of death and guilt? Would he ever awaken from a night's sleep without the bitter taste of loss in his mouth?

As he ate a quick microwave dinner, the haunting images faded. In the past five days, the workers had been busy in the kitchen. The old wiring had been replaced and updated, as had the plumbing.

New appliances were now in place and the old paint that had covered the cabinets had been sanded away to reveal the lustrous oak beneath. There was still a lot of work to be done in here, but when it was all finished, the kitchen would be a showplace.

Caleb finished his meal, then went upstairs to the

master bedroom and bath. A moment later, standing beneath the hot spray of a shower, his thoughts turned to Erica.

A date. He was actually going on a date. He scrubbed the minty soap bar across his chest and shook his head in amazement. It had been a long time since he'd dated...since before his marriage to Judith. He hoped he didn't make some awful mistake, somehow manage to alienate or offend Erica Clemmons.

Dating Erica involved a tremendous gamble. If she decided she couldn't stand him, wanted nothing to do with him, then his involvement with Hannah would come to an end as well.

It probably would have been smarter for him to remain a friendly neighbor and nothing more. But the moment he'd seen Erica sitting in the booth at the restaurant, pleasure had rippled through him...a pleasure that he believed had nothing to do with her daughter. It had been the pure emotion of a particular man happy to see a particular woman.

His attraction to Erica frightened him just a little bit. He couldn't be sure how true it was. Would he still be attracted to her if she weren't Hannah's mother? If she wasn't part of a package deal, would he still be drawn to her? There was no way for him to separate her from Hannah, and that made it difficult for him to assess his attraction to her.

He leaned forward and lifted his face to the shower spray. It was too soon to know what was going on in his own head, too soon to try to sort out the emotions Erica and Hannah stirred inside him.

One day at a time, he told himself as he stepped out of the shower and grabbed a towel. How many days did it take to heal a heart? He shook his head ruefully. It sounded like the setup to a bad joke.

But it wasn't a joke and Caleb didn't know the answer. He only knew that the thought of spending the evening with Erica invigorated him, made him both nervous and exhilarated....

Chapter 5

"Erica, this is the fourth time you've called in the last two hours," Sherry said with a sigh of exasperation. "Hannah is fine and perfectly satisfied. Just like she was the last time you called...and the time before that...and the—"

"Okay, I'm sorry. I'll admit, I'm a little bit neurotic." Erica waited for Sherry to protest this self-assessment, but Sherry remained loudly silent.

Erica looked at her wristwatch. A quarter after seven. She fought a rising sense of panic as she realized Caleb would be arriving in the next fifteen minutes. "If it's any consolation, I probably won't have time to call you again before he gets here."

"What are you wearing?"

Erica looked at her bed, where no less than a dozen

different outfits were tossed helter-skelter, then gazed downward. "At the moment, I'm clad in a white bra and panties."

"Great!" Sherry laughed. "That should move things right along."

"Ha, ha," Erica replied dryly. She sighed. "I'm having trouble deciding what to wear."

"That's odd, isn't it?" Amusement lit Sherry's voice. "I mean, why is what you're wearing a big deal if this is nothing more than just two neighbors sharing transportation to a movie?" She didn't wait for a reply. "Wear that pastel green dress that you wore two weeks ago when we met for lunch. It's casual but attractive, and unless you want to greet him in your bra and panties, you'd better hang up and get into it right now."

"Okay...kiss Hannah for me." With these final words, Erica hung up.

What she wanted to do was greet Caleb at the door in her oversized terry bathrobe and fuzzy slippers, cancel the date due to a strange ailment that had suddenly appeared. She wanted to crawl into bed and pull the covers over her head, hide from the attractive neighbor who both excited and confused her.

And what was it about the man that excited and confused her? Those blue eyes of his warmed her whenever they lingered on her, yet filled her with curiosity as she sensed shadows beneath their blue depths. His sense of humor delighted her as his patience and gentleness with Hannah awed her.

He confused her because she was drawn to him and didn't want to be, and she knew there were things about him, about his life, that she didn't know.

It's just a movie, she chided herself as she pulled the green dress off a hanger. A movie shared in the company of a neighbor. She was foolish to be so nervous. It was ridiculous to feel as if she were sixteen years old and this was her very first date.

She had been a wife, was a mother, she'd left dating and teenage angst behind a long time ago. She survived abandonment by her father, desertion by her husband and lived through the near death of her daughter. Surely she could handle a single dutch date with one handsome Caleb McMann.

By the time she was ready, she'd managed to put her anxiety behind. She would be pleasant to Caleb, would enjoy seeing the movie and that would be the end of it. Nothing more. Nothing less. Just a simple evening out.

Her doorbell rang at precisely seven-thirty and a renewed burst of apprehension fluttered in her stomach. She grabbed her purse, drew in a deep, cleansing breath, then opened the door to greet Caleb.

"All ready," she said briskly. She stepped out on the porch and pulled the door closed behind her.

"Great," he replied.

Together they walked toward his car parked in the driveway. When they got to the car, he opened the passenger door for her and she slid in.

As he walked around the front of the car to the

driver side, she noticed how his jeans clung to the length of his legs and cupped his shapely behind. The navy dress shirt hugged his broad shoulders and the tail of the shirt was neatly tucked into the jeans, emphasizing his lean waist and hips.

He slid behind the wheel and fumbled with his keys. Finding the correct one, he flashed her a quick smile, then started the engine and pulled out of the driveway.

For a few minutes neither of them spoke and Erica was aware of a strange tension radiating in the air. If she didn't know better, she would think he was as nervous as she.

She didn't want him to be nervous. That gave too much importance to the evening. It was bad enough that she felt a ridiculous case of the jitters. "How's the work on your house coming along?" she asked, more for conversation than from some desperate need to know.

"Good. You'll have to come over and take a look. I'm anxious to show off the progress to somebody."

She nodded, although she knew there was no way in this lifetime she would volunteer to enter his home. Somehow she knew in doing so they would muddle the boundaries she wanted to keep with this man.

Within minutes they arrived at the theater. As she'd told him earlier, she paid for her ticket and he paid for his own.

"Are you a front-row sitter, or a back-row?" he asked as they entered the dimly-lit theater.

"Middle of the center section," she replied.

"Ah," he said, a twinkle in his eyes. "Psychologically, that's very telling."

"Telling how?" she asked as they sank into seats directly in the middle of the center section. She didn't want to look at him. His navy shirt deepened the blue of his eyes, making them...making him impossibly sexy.

"There have been many scientific studies done on the subject. People who sit right up front want to be as close to the action as possible. They're risk-takers. People who choose to sit in the back want to remain distant, removed."

Despite her reluctance to look at him, she did. In the semidarkness his eyes gleamed teasingly. "But the ones who sit in the middle are terminal fence-sitters, unable to commit to anything."

"That's the biggest pile of hooey I've ever heard," she retorted. She shifted positions so his warm thigh wasn't pressing against her. "Psychological study, indeed. You just made that up."

He laughed, a low, deep chuckle that sent an unexpected rivulet of warmth shooting up her spine. "Busted," he agreed. "But it sounded scientific, didn't it?"

She grinned. "Like I said, it sounded like a pile of hooey."

"Before we get all settled in and the movie starts, what's your pleasure? Popcorn? Soda? Candy? A movie can't be fully appreciated without the benefits of junk food."

"Nothing for me," she replied, then took a deep grateful breath as he left to return to the concession stand in the lobby.

She'd only been sitting next to him mere minutes, but already her senses swam with the scent of him. He smelled of cool streams and fresh sunshine, and an underlying clean, male fragrance. Definitely pleasant. Definitely evocative and unsettling.

She smiled ruefully, wondering if she would have been more comfortable if he'd smelled of dirty sweat socks.

While he was gone, Erica took the opportunity to look around at their fellow moviegoers. The showing of the classic had not brought in much of a crowd and none of the younger set.

Several elderly couples were sitting down front and nobody sat behind Erica. Another smile curved her lips as she thought of Caleb's supposed scientific hypothesis.

She had a feeling the elderly couples sitting up front were there because of failing eyesight rather than from any desire to take risks. One couple in particular held her attention. The man had his arm around the lady's shoulders, and their heads were together as they whispered to each other.

It was easy to guess that they were married, had probably been married for nearly fifty years. Erica had once held dreams of silver and gold anniversaries, of sharing secrets and dreams with the man she'd pledged her heart to, but fate had decreed that she'd live her life differently.

She had adjusted to living without a soul mate, without a spouse. She had resigned herself to the fact that she would probably always be alone, but that didn't mean she didn't occasionally entertain a small, wistful hope for things to be different.

"Please tell me you're going to help me eat this," Caleb whispered as he returned to his seat. He held a container of popcorn the size of a small washtub. "If I eat this all by myself, you'll have to roll me out of here."

Erica laughed. "I might have a bite or two." She relaxed somewhat, realizing that she could no longer smell Caleb's pleasant scent. All she could smell was buttery popcorn.

As the lights dimmed and the coming attractions flashed on the screen, Erica settled back in her seat and focused her attention on the big screen.

It Happened One Night was definitely her favorite movie and she normally got completely caught up in the story, but this time was different. Normally, she immediately lost herself in watching love bloom on the screen, safely and vicariously living through the characters what she would never again chance for herself.

But this time she was far too aware of Caleb next to her. His shoulder touched hers, and his thigh would occasionally bump into hers. The space the seats provided seemed to shrink, encouraging an intimacy that was both thrilling and frightening.

It had been years since she'd been close enough to a man to smell his scent, feel his warmth and there was a part of her, a part she'd nearly forgotten, that was enjoying Caleb's nearness.

She steeled herself against the pleasure, knowing better than to trust it. It had been these same kinds of feelings that had once drawn her to her husband. And they hadn't been enough to keep her husband by her side.

The memory of Chuck's desertion left a bitter taste in her mouth. She'd handled it, managed to put it far behind her. She'd become stronger for it. Strong enough, smart enough to know she never, ever wanted to give any man that kind of power over her again. No man would ever work his way into her heart, only to leave her aching and alone. Never again.

As Caleb nudged the popcorn container toward her, she smiled at him, buoyed by the strength that suddenly flowed through her.

She could be his friend and not get entangled any deeper. She could be his neighbor and not cross the boundaries of neighborliness. Granted, he was handsome and smelled good, he was nice and had a wicked, wonderful smile, but she wasn't some pathetic, weak woman eager to gain a man in her life.

Been there, done that, she thought to herself. She had experienced the heartbreak of abandonment.

Thankfully, Hannah had been too young for Chuck's desertion to have left any real, lasting scars.

But Hannah had enough scars—real physical scars—and the last thing Erica would ever do was bring a man into her life who might add to them.

Grabbing another handful of the buttery popcorn, Erica once again directed her total attention to the romance unfolding on the screen. Vicariously…it was the smartest, safest way to experience a romance.

Caleb found himself observing Erica watching the movie. Again and again his gaze was drawn to her, the classic on the screen forgotten as he found pleasure in watching her features register reaction to the movie.

Earlier that evening, when she'd first opened her door to greet him, he'd felt like an adolescent schoolboy experiencing his very first date.

Painful self-awareness had flooded through him as he gazed at her beauty. He'd suddenly felt as if his arms and legs were too long, had a fear his voice might crack and he just might say something stupid. Thankfully, he'd managed to put the momentary teenage flashback behind.

He cast her another surreptitious glance. She looked like one of those after-dinner mints in the pale green dress, as if she would melt in his mouth and leave a sweet, sugary aftertaste.

Dangerous thoughts. He grabbed a handful of the popcorn and tried desperately to focus his attention on the screen. But it seemed as if all the surroundings conspired against him. How could he focus on the charms of Claudette Colbert when all he could smell was the exotic scent of Erica?

He'd told a little white lie when he'd said this movie was one of his favorites. He'd never seen it before. He hadn't been much of a moviegoer until Katie had turned four, but from then on, every Saturday father and daughter had gone to see whatever children's movie was playing at the local theaters.

A whole new world had opened to Caleb, the world of talking pigs and flying ants, a world he'd loved sharing with his daughter.

He shoved away thoughts of Katie. He didn't want to think about the tragic circumstances that had brought him here, to this place and time with this particular woman.

He didn't want to think of the past, or the future. He didn't want to delve into the question of what, exactly he was doing. Tonight he just wanted to be a normal man, enjoying the company of a lovely neighbor.

They whispered occasionally, pointing out something on the screen, and Caleb relished the momentary, pseudo-intimacy that came from the movie-theater setting and the whispers in the dark.

By the time the movie was over, Caleb was fully at ease, no longer worrying about what he was doing with Erica, or why he was so attracted to her. He sensed as the movie had progressed that she had relaxed too.

Several times their hands had met in the popcorn, and the smile she'd flashed him had seemed genuine and without any underlying stress. He'd felt her tension when he'd initially picked her up, knew that she had been manipulated into agreeing to coming in the first place.

"How about we stop somewhere and get a cup of coffee?" he suggested when the movie had ended and they were leaving the theater. "It's early...not quite ten o'clock."

"Oh, thanks, but I really should get right home. I need to pick up Hannah from Sherry's." She flashed him an apologetic look. "I...I never leave her with anyone. This is the first time in a long while that we've been apart for any length of time." Her cheeks burned a becoming pink. "I know it sounds neurotic, but with good reason."

"Erica," he touched her arm lightly. "You don't owe me any explanations."

"But, I do. I mean, I'd like to explain it to you." The color in her cheeks intensified and Caleb felt a thick dread course through him. He didn't want her to tell him about Hannah, because then he would have to tell her about Katie.

They reached his car and he opened the passenger door, trying to think of something, anything that might halt the conversation he knew they were about to have.

And yet, at the same time there was a part of him that was pleased that she felt as if she could confide in him. He slid behind the steering wheel with a curious sense of anticipation and resignation.

Neither of them spoke until he'd started the engine and pulled out of the theater parking lot. "Look, rather than taking you home, then you having to get into your car to pick up Hannah, why don't I just swing by Sherry's house and collect Hannah?"

She hesitated a moment. "You sure you don't mind?"

"No problem, as long as you can give me directions to Sherry's house."

"Okay," she agreed and settled back in the seat.

Caleb breathed a sigh of relief, hoping he'd managed to circumvent any discussion of Hannah's heart condition. He cast her a quick glance. She stared out the window, a thoughtful frown creasing her forehead.

Finally she spoke. "Have you ever wondered how fate chooses who will run through life seemingly without heartache, with little strife, and who will carry horribly heavy burdens and be forever scarred?"

He looked at her in surprise. He hadn't been expecting a discussion about the fickleness of fate. He wasn't sure which of them might teach the other about heavy burdens and scars. They'd both had more than their share. "I try not to think too much about fate," he replied truthfully. "I figure the best you can do is get through it all one day at a time and not try to analyze why things happen to you."

"They say you're never given more than you can handle."

He smiled. "Now, *that's* a bunch of hooey."

She laughed, the sound wonderfully feminine and musical. "I completely agree." She pointed to the corner in the distance. "Turn left at the light," she instructed.

"Have you and Sherry been friends for long?" he asked.

"It feels like forever. We went through high school, then college together."

"She seems nice."

Erica nodded. "Sherry is ambitious, driven, and at times a bit of a kook, but she's the nicest person you ever want to meet. She's helped me through a lot of things in the past. Sherry's always been there to offer all kinds of support." She pointed again. "Turn right at the next corner."

Caleb turned onto the tree-lined street, slowing down as Erica pointed to a house on the right. "This is it," she said. Caleb pulled along the side of the curb and shut off the engine, then both he and Erica got out of the car and headed for the attractive ranch house.

Erica knocked on the door and they waited only a moment before Hannah answered. "Oh Mommy, are you here already?" Dismay was evident in the little girl's voice.

"I'm glad to see you, too," Erica replied dryly.

Hannah giggled, then pulled her mom down and gave her a quicksilver kiss on the cheek. "Wanna see the picture I made?"

Erica and Caleb followed her through the living room and into a light, airy kitchen. Sherry stood at the sink, obviously doing paint cleanup. "Hey, you two, you're earlier than I expected. How was the movie?" She reached for a towel to dry her hands.

"Good. How did things go here?" Erica asked.

"We've had a terrific time. We ate Chinese food and finger painted. We ate popcorn and finger painted. We ate pizza and finger painted," Sherry explained.

Erica groaned. "I hope you're on call later if she gets sick from eating too much."

"I won't get sick, Mommy. I had fun, fun, fun! The bestest time ever." Hannah danced up and down. "Now, look at my pictures. Look Mr. Man, here's a picture of our tree house. See, you and me are in it and we're looking out the window."

Caleb studied the picture with interest. "What a great picture," he exclaimed as the little girl preened.

"You can have it," she said. "You can put it on your 'frigerator."

"Thank you, Hannah. It's the best picture I've ever had."

He watched as Hannah showed Erica the other pictures she'd painted. As much as he loved watching Hannah, tonight his gaze was drawn again and again to Erica. Her hair was a waterfall of silky brown and his fingers itched to stroke the shiny strands. A man could get lost in the gleaming length of her hair, just as he could drown in the lagoon blue of her eyes.

"Pack it up, kiddo," Erica said. "It's past time for you to get home and into bed."

"Let's just stay a little longer," Hannah protested. "I don't want to go to bed yet." At the same time she was saying the words, she rubbed her eyes, her tiredness obvious.

Caleb scooped her up in his arms. "Come on, little one. It's not only past your bedtime, but it's way past mine." He tickled her, then set her back on the floor.

She giggled and gathered up her paintings as Erica threw Caleb a look of gratitude.

Within minutes they'd said their goodbyes and were back in the car. They'd only gotten a block from Sherry's place before Hannah was sound asleep in the back seat.

"I think somebody had a little too much fun," Caleb observed.

Erica smiled. "Yes, she went out like a light." She sighed softly. "It was probably good for her...being away from me for a little while."

Caleb heard a touch of sadness in her voice. He reached out and lightly touched her hand. "I guess letting them go is the most difficult thing parents do."

She nodded. "It's been just me and Hannah for so long. Before, that was always enough for both of us. But I guess she's getting to the age where she needs other people besides me."

"And you need other people besides her," Caleb replied.

"Oh, I don't know about that. I'm satisfied the way things are," she protested.

"But, things never stay the way they are. Every day Hannah will get older, more independent. You can't build your life around a little girl, because little girls grow up."

Erica laughed, although there was an edge to the laughter. "You sound like Sherry."

"Great minds think alike," he said with a grin.

"Tell me, when was the first time you saw *It Happened One Night*?"

"An unsubtle attempt to change the topic of conversation?"

"Exactly."

He laughed. "I have a confession to make. Tonight was the first time I ever saw the movie."

She stared at him in surprise. "But you said it was one of your favorites."

"A tiny white lie. I wanted to go to the movies with you."

She didn't reply, and he wasn't sure whether he'd offended her or not. He turned into her driveway and shut off the engine.

"So, did you like the show?" she asked finally.

He hesitated a moment, unable to answer truthfully. He couldn't tell her that he'd found it impossible to concentrate on the story line, that instead he'd enjoyed watching her, seeing the emotions play on her features. "It was very good," he finally answered.

She nodded, as if satisfied, then smiled. "Thank you, Caleb."

"For what? We went dutch."

Her smile deepened. "For the popcorn and the adult company." She opened her car door and stepped out.

He hurriedly got out as well. "Why don't I carry the little munchkin in for you?" He didn't want the evening to end. He was enjoying her smile, their conversation, the very scent of her.

"That isn't necessary," she protested. "I can get her."

He sensed a sudden tension in Erica, as if he'd overstepped some invisible boundary she'd created. "I really don't mind," he said.

"And I appreciate that, but she's my daughter. I'll handle it." Erica opened the backdoor.

"She'll be heavy," Caleb said, unsure about what had happened but knowing that Erica had retreated. "I can't believe we're going to have our first fight over who is going to carry a sleeping child."

She didn't reply, but bent down to unbuckle the seat belt. She pulled Hannah into her arms, staggering slightly beneath the weight. "Let me," Caleb insisted, holding out his arms.

Erica hesitated a moment, then allowed him to take the little girl. "Okay," she relented.

Hannah's arms automatically sought his neck and she curled herself against him.

A bittersweet ache pierced him. So like Katie. How many times had Caleb carried his sleeping daughter to bed after a night out? How many times had he felt the warmth of her chubby arms wrapped around his neck, a whisper of little-girl breath in the hollow of his neck? A hundred times? A thousand? No matter how many, it hadn't been enough.

Erica unlocked the front door and guided him through the small living room and into Hannah's room where the window air conditioner hummed loudly, but made the temperature pleasantly cool.

Erica quickly pulled down the sheet and Caleb placed the sleeping child on the bed. He stepped back and watched as Erica skillfully removed her shoes, then tucked her in and kissed her forehead. Since Hannah was wearing sweats, Erica decided they'd be comfortable enough to sleep in. She preferred not to disturb her by putting her in her pajamas.

Kissing a forehead, tucking in a blanket…simple pleasures taken for granted. Caleb had a desire to grab hold of Erica, to warn her, to make certain she cherished each and every moment she had with her child. They were fleeting moments, destined to be stolen by tragic accidents, the whims of fate or by the mere normalcy of a passing childhood.

"How about some coffee?" Erica suggested as they left the bedroom.

"Sure," he agreed, both surprised and pleased by the offer.

They went into the kitchen, where she motioned him to the table, then turned on the ceiling fan to stir the heat in the room. "Only a couple more days of the fans, then we'll have air-conditioning throughout the house," she said as she made the coffee.

"That will be nice for you."

"It's nothing short of miraculous," she replied. "I didn't think Stanley would ever spring for central air." The coffeepot gurgled and hissed, the fresh brew filling the kitchen with its delicious scent.

Caleb found himself relaxing as he hadn't done in a very long time. A sense of peace flowed through him, a peace that had been elusive for the last year or so of his life. Nothing like sharing coffee with a beautiful, gracious woman to set things right with the world, he thought.

With each minute of the evening that had passed, he'd found himself more and more drawn to Erica. He liked the sound of her laughter and the way a tiny wrinkle appeared in her forehead when she was deep in thought.

It had been a long time since Caleb had entertained any kind of interest in a woman, especially a sexual interest, but as he'd sat next to Erica during the movie, he'd felt longing unfurl inside him. As he watched her reach into a cabinet for two cups, the short skirt displaying her slender, tanned legs, the longing grew stronger.

He wanted to tangle his hands in the length of her hair, dance his lips along the column of her neck, taste her lips with his own. He could easily imagine unzipping the back of her dress, feeling the warmth of her skin as each inch was revealed to his view. Heat soared through him and for a moment he found it difficult to breathe.

He tore his gaze from her and instead focused on the refrigerator, which was decorated with several of Hannah's art handiwork.

"Here we are," Erica said as she placed two cups of coffee on the table. She sat across from him, making it impossible for him to look at anything but her. She wrapped her hands around the cup, then looked at him solemnly. "I'd like to explain to you, tell you about Hannah."

Caleb's heart sank. He didn't want to have this conversation with her. It was too soon…Erica might not understand if he told her about Katie. The only other alternative was to say nothing about his daughter…but he knew that would be unfair.

Panic set in as he struggled for the best way to handle things. He didn't know what to do. But, worse than that was the overwhelming feeling that no matter what he did, it was going to be horribly wrong.

Chapter 6

Erica wasn't sure why, exactly, it was so important to her that Caleb know about Hannah's illness. She wasn't one to indiscriminately share private pieces of her life with anyone, but despite her reluctance to get romantically involved, something about Caleb made her want to share this part of their lives.

"Hannah was born with a malfunctioning heart," she began. "I could give you all the medical jargon and terminology, but it probably wouldn't mean anything to you. The bottom line is her heart wasn't working right and the doctors didn't believe she was strong enough for surgery. She was given only weeks to live."

"That must have been really tough," Caleb said softly.

Memories assailed Erica...the tremendous high of giving birth, followed by the pronouncement of doom. Even now, the memory of the doctor's face as he'd explained Hannah's problems remained burned in her mind. He'd been compassionate and his eyes had radiated sadness, and Erica had felt as if her whole world had shattered into pieces as he'd explained the tragic outlook.

She shoved the memory away, knowing that even now it had the power to move her to tears. "When the doctors told us Hannah's prognosis, Chuck and I coped with it in diametrically opposed ways. Chuck turned off emotionally. He didn't want anything to do with Hannah. He didn't want to touch her or hold her. He didn't even want to look at her." She paused a moment, remembering how angry she'd been with the man she had married.

Drawing a deep breath, she continued, "I, on the other hand, couldn't get enough of her. I figured if I only had a week or two with her, I was going to cram a lifetime of loving into the brief time we had together."

She paused again, this time to take a sip of her coffee. "I realize now Chuck was afraid to love her, afraid of the inevitable loss." She straightened in her chair and smiled at Caleb. "But Hannah astounded everyone. She not only survived the first month of her life, she thrived. But Chuck never got past his fear. By the time Hannah had her first surgery, he'd left and never looked back."

"His loss," Caleb observed.

"My sentiments exactly," she agreed. Briefly, she told Caleb about the many surgeries, the hopes, the defeats of the last five years.

She tried to keep her story succinct, as emotionless as possible. She didn't want to bore him, but wanted him to understand all they had been through in the quest to keep Hannah alive. "Over the next couple of years, after dozens of surgeries, the doctors had finally exhausted all their resources and they told me the only thing that would save her life would be a heart transplant."

"And?"

"And almost a year ago, she had one." Erica felt the tremendous smile that stretched her lips, a smile that came from her very soul. "And since that time, it's as if she not only got a new heart, but new life as well. She's healthier now than she's ever been before."

"I'm so glad." Caleb's eyes shone with intensity. "I hope she lives a long and healthy life. She's a special little girl."

"I think she will," Erica said softly. "I think Hannah must have a very special mission here on earth to fulfill." She shrugged and laughed, as if to lighten the conversation. "Anyway, I'm telling you all this so you'll understand why I'm overly cautious where Hannah is concerned. I'm so accustomed to her being sick, it's taking some adjustment on my part now that she's well."

"That's understandable."

She smiled at him gratefully. "According to Sherry, I'm a neurotic mess."

He laughed, the sound deep and pleasant and stroking forgotten chords inside Erica. "I don't think so," he said.

"Maybe you just don't know me that well yet," she retorted.

"Then I reserve the right to state my opinion after I know you better."

"If I *let* you get to know me better," she teased. Flirting. She was amazed to realize she was actually flirting with him. And even though she was still terrified by the feelings he awakened in her, being playful with Caleb felt wonderful. She'd forgotten how good it felt to be attracted to a man, and to want him to be attracted to her.

He leaned forward, his silvery-blue eyes almost hypnotic as they gazed at her intently. "Maybe I won't give you a chance to deny me knowing you better. When I turn on the McMann charm, you won't be able to refuse me anything." His voice was light, teasing and she recognized the fact that he was flirting with her.

She grinned. "Be sure and let me know when you turn it on. I'd hate to be the first woman who didn't succumb to the McMann charm."

He laughed and sat back in his chair. "Don't worry, I promise I'll give you fair warning." Although his words were light, there was something in his eyes, a sweet longing that touched a mirrored emotion inside her.

"More coffee?" She jumped up from the chair, deciding the teasing had gone on long enough.

She still was unsure if Caleb McMann was a prince or a frog and she wasn't ready to take a chance again. She refused to consider risking her heart—or Hannah's—to heartbreak.

She topped off his cup, then gestured toward the living room. "Why don't we go in there where we'll be more comfortable?"

"Fine with me," he agreed.

Moments later they were both seated on the sofa, a safe two feet apart from each other. Even with the distance between them, Erica was acutely aware of the appealing scent of his cologne, the masculinity that exuded from him and filled the room.

How easy it would be for her to lean forward, bridge the space between them and place her lips against his. It had been years since she'd thought of kissing a man, but at the moment she was having trouble thinking of anything else.

Caleb had a nice mouth, one that looked as if it had been made just for kissing. She could almost imagine the softness, the evocative heat of his lips against hers.

"So, tell me about the work you've done on the house," she said, desperate for conversation that would take her mind off his kissable mouth.

He set his coffee cup down on the table and leaned forward. As he launched into a description of the renovations, it was easy to tell it was a subject near and dear to his heart.

His eyes shone and his features were lit with an appealing animation as he talked about the beautiful wood he'd found beneath layers of paint, the hardwood floors beneath the old carpeting. His voice was deep and mellow, washing over her like a half-remembered pleasant dream.

She'd once had fantasies about lying in bed next to a special man, listening to him as he shared his work, his dreams, his goals. She'd dreamed of that man's voice lulling her to sleep with sweet nighttime murmurs, or stroking flames into her soul with husky words of passion.

She set her cup down next to his and gave herself a mental shake. What was wrong with her? Why was she fantasizing, not only about kissing Caleb, but lying in bed with him, making love with him? With studied concentration, she managed to focus on what he was saying rather than old, discarded fantasies she no longer believed in.

"Sounds like the house is going to be a true show-place when you get finished with it," she said.

"I hope somebody thinks so. I figure another month or so and it will be ready to put back on the market."

She looked at him in surprise. "You're going to sell it?"

He frowned thoughtfully. "Probably. I never really intended to keep it. It's too much house for a man all alone."

"Does that mean you'll be going back to Chicago?" She was surprised to discover that the thought of him leaving bothered her. Funny, two days ago his presence had bothered her; now the thought of him no longer being around bothered her. She was nothing if not perverse.

"I don't know." He shrugged and looked away. "I'm sort of taking things one day at a time for the moment. I haven't made any plans to stay or to go."

Erica pulled her feet up beneath her on the sofa and leaned back into the cushions. "I'd buy the house in a minute if I could afford it." She smiled ruefully. "Unfortunately, I couldn't even manage the mortgage on that tree house you're building."

He laughed. "If and when I sell, I'll make sure it's written into the buyer's contract that Hannah gets visitation rights to the tree house."

"She'll haunt you forever if you don't," Erica replied, also laughing. Her laughter ended in a yawn and she tried to stifle it with the back of her hand.

"Maybe we should call it a night," Caleb said. He smiled teasingly. "When I make a woman yawn, it's time to exit." He stood and grabbed his cup.

"Leave it," she said, also rising. "I'll get them as I go to bed."

She walked with him to the door and together they stepped out onto her tiny porch. The night was still except for a faint breeze that carried the scent of nearby honeysuckle. As they faced each other, with only the light filtering from her living room to illuminate the darkness, Erica's heart quickened at his nearness.

"I enjoyed the evening," he said. His eyes twinkled as his gaze lingered on her. "Although I must confess, I started the evening with a very bad case of nerves. It has been years since I've gone to a movie with a lovely lady...especially dutch treat."

Erica smiled, the thought of him being nervous oddly charming. "I was a little anxious, too," she confessed. "But we did all right, didn't we?"

He stepped closer to her. "We did so well, I wouldn't mind repeating the pleasure."

She wanted to tell him no, to say that she didn't want a relationship, that she didn't believe in happily-ever-afters. She wanted to tell him that she refused to be hurt again. But he's only asking for another movie date, the rational part of her brain insisted. He isn't asking for forever.

Before she had a chance to say anything, he dipped his head and claimed her lips. At first the kiss was soft, tentative, as if he were unsure what her response might be.

When she didn't step back, didn't pull away, he wrapped his arms around her waist and deepened the kiss. Without volition, her arms moved up, her hands clasping him behind his neck.

Their bodies pressed together as passion soared and his tongue touched hers. Erica's head reeled dizzily as heat enveloped her, a heat that began in her center and radiated throughout her body.

Her fingers splayed at his nape, enjoying the crisp feel of his hair, the solid muscle of his neck. Somewhere in the back of her mind, she knew they were treading on dangerous ground, crossing a boundary she'd been determined they wouldn't.

But breaking away from the kiss, stepping back from the sweet warmth of his arms, seemed utterly impossible. Rather, she wanted to linger in his embrace, taste the fires of his kiss for an indefinite amount of time.

She could feel his body against hers, the firm chest against her soft breasts, his lean legs pressed taut against hers. Her heart tattooed a rapid rhythm as she felt the full extent of his arousal.

The physical evidence of his desire caused stark reality to pierce the fog of passion his kiss had produced. She broke the kiss and stepped back, her legs slightly shaky with the desire that still coursed through her.

"You taste just like I imagined you would." His voice was husky and his eyes held the gleam of a million stars.

Her cheeks warmed and she averted her gaze from him, afraid that if she peered into his eyes for too long, she and Caleb would fall back into another kiss...one she might not have the strength to stop. "I probably taste like buttery popcorn and coffee," she said with an uncomfortable little laugh.

"A compelling combination." He reached out and drew his index finger down her cheek, then dropped his hand. "Good night, Erica."

"'Night, Caleb.''

She watched as he went down the steps and got back into his car. She stood on the porch until he'd backed out of the driveway and disappeared down the street, his car's taillights swallowed by the darkness of the night.

Still she lingered. Wrapping her arms around her shoulders, she leaned against the front door and drew in a deep breath of the fragrant night air. She would never again smell the sweet scent of honeysuckle and not think of her first exciting, wonderful kiss with Caleb.

First kiss. Why had she not thought *only* kiss? It was as if she was already anticipating repeating the pleasure, as if she knew in her heart the kiss they'd just shared was only the first of many. Heat swept through her.

You'd better hang on to your heart, she warned herself firmly as she left the porch and went back into the house. She wasn't about to fall back into hopeless fantasies of love. She couldn't take another bond, another bout of broken promises and unfulfilled dreams. It was better not to dream at all.

Caleb had been clear about the fact that he didn't know if he intended to remain in St. Louis or go back to Chicago. It would be crazy for her to fall into any sort of intimate relationship with him, even crazier to allow Hannah to hope for any kind of bond with a man who would probably only manage to break her fragile heart.

Erica had no idea yet if Caleb McMann was a prince or a frog and she wasn't willing to chance her heart or her daughter's in order to find out for sure.

Caleb sat on the floor of the large, airy bedroom, carefully sanding the combined oak window seat and toy box he'd finished building the night before.

He paused to run his hand along the edge, checking for rough wood that might produce splinters. Smooth as glass.

Satisfied, he sat back on his haunches and looked around the room. He had no idea what this second-floor space had originally been, but the moment he'd seen it, he'd known it was a perfect bedroom for a child.

Caleb had spent the two weeks since he'd moved into the house making it even more perfect. He'd not only built the low, easily accessible window seats that opened to provide toy storage, but he'd also added two solid oak bookcases with wide, deep shelving.

The masterpiece was the solid structure he had built against one wall, which not only provided bunkbeds for sleeping, but also a jungle gym for hours of playing pleasure.

It was a room made for a princess...a room his princess would never play in, where she would never sleep. The pain that swept through him at the thought of Katie less intense than it had always been before. Was time finally muting the agony? Making the loss liveable? The pain of her loss would always be with him; he just hoped it would eventually become manageable.

Deciding to take a lunch break, he stood and stretched, then headed for the kitchen.

It took him only minutes to slap together a sandwich and sit down at the table. From the living room came the sounds of the painters he'd hired, their conversation punctuated by the noise of their paint rollers as they transformed the walls from old and faded to new and bright.

He should have told her. The thought came unbidden, as it had a hundred times in the two days since he and Erica had gone to the movies.

And then came the sharp stab of guilt. He should have told her about Katie. He should have told her about Katie's heart.

He'd meant to. As she'd explained to him about Hannah's health problems, the confession had taken form in his head, but it had never made it to his mouth.

Fear had kept him silent…the fear that she'd send him away, the fear that he'd never get to spend time with her again, never get to kiss her again.

The kiss. Even now, two days after the fact, the thought of their kiss sent rivulets of warmth up his spine, a tingling of desire through his veins. He hadn't expected this sharp, intense reaction to kissing her, he hadn't expected the overwhelming need and want that had washed over him.

He realized now his desire for Erica was a very separate need from his wish to spend additional time with Hannah. Being with Hannah helped assuage the devastating emptiness that Katie's death had left behind. Seeing the little girl so filled with life, cheeks flushed with health, somehow made the ache less intense. Besides, Hannah was a delightful little girl who had easily managed to capture Caleb's affection.

Being with Erica had awakened very different needs, needs he'd believed he no longer possessed. When Judith had died, he'd decided that having Katie in his life was enough.

He hadn't pursued other women, hadn't dated or even dreamed that a day would come when the loneliness inside him might make him feel differently.

Erica made him think that perhaps he'd been wrong to shut himself off so completely from the idea of loving again. Judith wouldn't have wanted him to spend his life alone.

Just before Judith's death, she'd made him promise her two things: first, that he would remarry, and second, that he would take care of Katie. He'd failed miserably at both promises.

He wasn't sure specifically what his feelings were where Erica was concerned. He only knew he enjoyed her company, admired her strength, and felt a strong physical desire for her.

You should have told her the truth, that little inner voice returned to nag at him. *You owe it to her. She has to know sooner or later.*

He frowned and finished the last bite of his sandwich. He should tell her...now, before their relationship developed any further.

A knock on the back door made him jump in surprise. He hurried to answer and was surprised to see Hannah standing on his back porch.

"Hi, munchkin," he greeted her. "Where's your mother?"

She pushed past him into the kitchen, her big brown eyes snapping with childish anger. "She's at home. I runned away." She took a seat at the table, appearing as comfortable as if she'd been in his home, sat at his table a hundred times before. "You got any cookies?" she asked.

Caleb nodded. "Did you tell your mother that you were running away?" he asked as he got out a package of chocolate-chip cookies.

"No. I sneaked out the window in my room. Can I have a glass of milk with these?"

"Sure." Caleb poured the milk then joined her at the table. "Why did you run away?"

Hannah frowned and chewed a cookie thoughtfully. "My dream friend says I'm too big for naps, and I don't want to take them anymore, but Mommy says I have to 'cause of my heart. I hate naps, so, I runned away."

Caleb hid a smile, remembering how Katie had always hated to nap. "Maybe we should call and let your mother know you're gone. Running away really doesn't count unless you tell your mom." Caleb knew how worried Erica would be if she decided to check on her napping child and found instead an empty bedroom.

Hannah scratched her cheek thoughtfully. "Okay. You can call her and tell her, but tell her I'm not ever coming home until I don't have to take any more naps."

Caleb got up from the table and used the kitchen phone to call Erica. "Hi, Erica," he said when she answered. An unexpected warmth washed through him at the sound of her voice. "I just wanted to let you know that Hannah has run away from home and is now sitting at my kitchen table."

"What?" It was obvious from Erica's reaction that she had no idea her daughter had defected out the window. "She's run away? Why?"

"She refuses to take another nap," he said, once again hiding a smile as Hannah nodded solemnly.

"Really?" Amusement lit Erica's voice, again creating a flood of warmth in Caleb as he imagined her lips curved into an appealing smile.

"She says she isn't coming home until you agree to no more naps."

Erica laughed. "That little stinker."

"I think maybe this is a dilemma that should be discussed over milk and cookies."

"I'll be right over."

She hung up and Caleb did the same, then turned to face Hannah. "Is she mad?" Hannah asked.

"She's coming over to talk with you."

"She didn't say anything about a time-out, did

she?'' Hannah said the word *time-out* as if it left a dreadful taste in her mouth.

Caleb rejoined her at the table. ''No, she didn't mention a time-out.''

''Good.'' She breathed a deep sigh of relief, then frowned again. ''I don't need naps no more. The doctor says I'm healthy as a horse.'' She tilted her head and looked at Caleb. ''I'd like to have a horse someday. Wouldn't that be nice?''

Caleb smiled. He'd learned a long time ago that conversations with children never followed any kind of pattern but a purely spontaneous one. From naps to horses in the space of a sentence.

''Hello?'' Erica's voice called from the back door.

''Come on in,'' Caleb replied.

She entered, ushering in a breeze of hot air and the scent that Caleb would forever associate with her…the scent of sweet, blooming flowers and fresh, clean rain. ''Hmm, chocolate chip…my favorite.'' She sat down in the chair between Hannah and Caleb and reached for one of the cookies in the center of the table.

She took a bite of the cookie, then smiled at Caleb. ''It's a gorgeous day, isn't it?''

''Beautiful,'' he agreed.

''Hard to believe it's already July. Summer will be over before we know it,'' Erica continued.

''Mommy!'' Hannah sighed in frustration, obviously piqued that the conversation wasn't revolving around her. ''I runned away.''

"Yes, that's what Caleb explained to me on the phone," Erica replied.

"I'm not coming home, Mommy, not until I don't have to take any more naps." Hannah raised her little chin rebelliously.

"Where will you live?" Erica asked.

It was obvious the question surprised Hannah. Her eyes opened wide and she looked from her mother to Caleb, then back again. "I'll live in the tree house."

"The tree house isn't ready yet," Caleb said. "I still have to put the windows in. Right now, if you live in it, when it rains you'll get wet. When the weather turns cold, you'll be cold."

"I don't care. I'll be cold so I don't have to take any more naps," Hannah replied stubbornly.

Erica exchanged a glance with Caleb, and for just a moment he felt as if he'd fallen into a world where the two of them were life partners, where they were sharing the parenting of the precocious little girl.

"Hannah, naps are good for you. It's when your body rests," Erica explained.

"My dream friend says we're too old for naps."

Erica frowned. "I wish I could have a talk with your dream friend."

"What about quiet time instead of naps?" Caleb suggested. He hoped he wasn't overstepping his bounds and sighed in relief as Erica nodded her encouragement.

"What do you mean?" Hannah eyed him suspiciously.

"Each afternoon, you could lie quietly and read a book, or maybe draw pictures, but you wouldn't have to actually take a nap," he explained.

"I think that sounds agreeable," Erica said.

Hannah studied her mom thoughtfully. "And we wouldn't call it nap time?"

"Nap time is for babies. Quiet time is for adults," Caleb said.

"And you're right," Erica said. "You aren't a baby any more."

Hannah finished the last bite of a cookie, then drained the milk from her glass. "Okay," she said as she swiped her upper lip with the back of her hand. "We can go home now."

Together the three of them stood and stepped out the back door. "'Bye, Mr. Man," Hannah said as she headed toward the gate of the fence that separated the two properties. "Thanks for the cookies."

Erica paused on the porch, her warm smile lighting all the shadows in Caleb's heart. "You handled that very well."

"So did you," he replied. "Let's hope all her childhood growing pains are handled as easily."

"Amen." She cocked her head, her gaze lingering on him. "We've planned a trip to the zoo for next Saturday. I thought I'd pack a picnic lunch and we'd spend the day there. Would you like to join us?"

He was thrilled by the invitation. "I can't think of anything I'd rather do."

"Then why don't we plan on going about ten."

"Sounds great. I'll be at your house at ten."

She nodded and started to leave, then turned back to him. "You really should have children someday, Caleb. You'd make a wonderful father."

Caleb was grateful that she immediately turned and walked back toward her house. He was grateful she couldn't see his tears. He was grateful she wouldn't know how her words had reopened the wounds he'd thought had begun to heal.

Chapter 7

"She's growing up," Erica said as Hannah raced ahead of them toward the monkey cages. Clad in a bright yellow sundress, the little girl looked like a piece of the sun whirling in the hot breeze.

"That's what children are supposed to do," Caleb said, his gaze as warm as the sun itself as it lingered on her.

"I know. But it's happening so fast. A year ago she was so fragile, so needy, and now I can't seem to keep up with her." Erica sighed, fighting off a tinge of depression that had been with her for the past week.

It had surprised her how quickly Hannah had jumped at the opportunity to spend time without her mother the night Erica and Caleb had gone to the movies. Hannah running away, rebelling against nap time had been further proof that the little girl was reaching out to life…reaching away from Erica.

Before, Erica had always been enough for Hannah. Now that was no longer the case. Hannah had begun to look outward, she'd begun to recognize there was a whole big world out there, a world outside of her mother.

Caleb threw an arm around her shoulders. "Relax, you still have a few years before she marries and leaves your home forever."

Erica laughed, surprised to discover how good, how utterly right his arm felt around her. He smelled like summer, a clean scent of sunshine, fresh air and a dash of masculine cologne. As always, he looked devastatingly handsome in his tight jeans and a short-sleeved blue T-shirt that made his eyes the color of blue ice, with just a hint of silver.

She was beginning to trust him, and that both frightened and thrilled her. It had been so long since she'd opened herself up to a man, allowed herself to be vulnerable and let the winds of chance guide her. She only hoped this time fate would be more kind than it had been in the past.

"Look Mommy! Look, Mr. Man!" Hannah squealed with delight as she watched the monkeys swinging through the trees, chattering with excitement. "Look at the little baby." Hannah pointed to a tiny monkey clinging to its mother's belly. She turned and eyed Erica in speculation. "I think you need to have a baby. I'd make a really good big sister."

Erica looked at her daughter in surprise. Never had Hannah expressed a desire for a sibling. "Honey...I can't...we're not...you're supposed to be married before you have a baby. I'm not married."

"But you could be. You could marry Mr. Man." Hannah smiled at them both, as if extremely pleased with her idea. "He'd make a very good daddy."

Caleb dropped his arm from around Erica's shoulders at the same time she stepped away from him. "Honey, it's not that simple," Erica said, her cheeks warming with embarrassment.

"How come?" Hannah placed her hands on her hips and stared at the two adults. "You get married, you have a baby and we all live happily ever after."

"How about we see the polar bears, eat some lunch and all live happily ever after?" Caleb suggested.

Hannah thought for a moment, then smiled. "Okay, let's go see the bears." She skipped ahead of them.

"Thanks," Erica said to Caleb.

"No problem." His eyes twinkled in amusement. "Leave it to kids to put their parents in awkward positions."

She looked at him curiously. "You talk like a man with experience."

"Actually, I..."

"Hannah, stay on this side of the fence," Erica yelled as she saw Hannah leaning over the protective railing that surrounded the bears' compound. "Sorry." She flashed an apologetic smile at Caleb. "You were saying?"

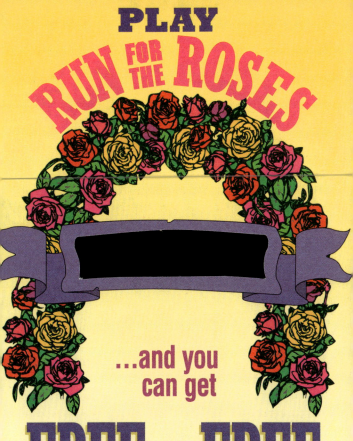

PLAY
RUN FOR THE ROSES

...and you
can get

FREE BOOKS and a FREE GIFT!

Turn the page and let the race begin!

PLAY

RUN

FOR THE

ROSES

and get

THREE FREE GIFTS!

HOW TO PLAY:

1. With a coin, carefully scratch off the silver box at the right. Then check the claim chart to see what we have for you — **2 FREE BOOKS** and a **FREE GIFT** — **ALL YOURS FREE!**

2. Send back the card and you'll receive two brand-new Silhouette Intimate Moments® novels. These books have a cover price of $4.50 each in the U.S. and $5.25 each in Canada, but they are yours to keep absolutely free.

3. There's no catch. You're under no obligation to buy anything. We charge nothing — ZERO — for your first shipment. And you don't have to make any minimum number of purchases — not even one!

4. The fact is, thousands of readers enjoy receiving books by mail from the Silhouette Reader Service™. They enjoy the convenience of home delivery...they like getting the best new novels at discount prices, BEFORE they're available in stores... and they love their *Heart to Heart* subscriber newsletter featuring author news, horoscopes, recipes, book reviews and much more!

5. We hope that after receiving your free books you'll want to remain a subscriber. But the choice is yours — to continue or cancel, any time at all! So why not take us up on our invitation, with no risk of any kind. You'll be glad you did!

Visit us online at

www.eHarlequin.com

This surprise mystery gift
Could be yours **FREE** –
When you play
RUN for the ROSES

Scratch Here
See Claim Chart

DETACH AND MAIL CARD TODAY!

RUN for the ROSES			Claim Chart
♔	♔	♔	**2 FREE BOOKS AND A MYSTERY GIFT!**
♔	♔		**1 FREE BOOK!**
♔			**TRY AGAIN!**

NAME (PLEASE PRINT CLEARLY)

ADDRESS

APT.#   CITY

STATE/PROV.   ZIP/POSTAL CODE

345 SDL C25A

245 SDL C245
(S-IM-OS-05/00)

The Silhouette Reader Service™ — Here's how it works:

Accepting your 2 free books and gift places you under no obligation to buy anything. You may keep the books and gift and return the shipping statement marked "cancel." If you do not cancel, about a month later we'll send you 6 additional novels and bill you just $3.80 each in the U.S., or $4.21 each in Canada, plus 25¢ delivery per book and applicable taxes if any.*
That's the complete price and — compared to cover prices of $4.50 each in the U.S. and $5.25 each in Canada — it's quite a bargain! You may cancel at any time, but if you choose to continue, every month we'll send you 6 more books, which you may either purchase at the discount price or return to us and cancel your subscription.

*Terms and prices subject to change without notice. Sales tax applicable in N.Y. Canadian residents will be charged applicable provincial taxes and GST.

If offer card is missing write to: Silhouette Reader Service, 3010 Walden Ave., P.O. Box 1867, Buffalo NY 14240-1867

BUSINESS REPLY MAIL
FIRST-CLASS MAIL   PERMIT NO. 717   BUFFALO, NY

POSTAGE WILL BE PAID BY ADDRESSEE

SILHOUETTE READER SERVICE
3010 WALDEN AVE
PO BOX 1867
BUFFALO NY 14240-9952

NO POSTAGE
NECESSARY
IF MAILED
IN THE
UNITED STATES

He shrugged. "It wasn't important."

She had the feeling he'd been about to tell her something...something important, but as she saw the guarded expression in his eyes, she knew the moment had passed and dismissed it from her mind.

Throughout the rest of the morning as they went from one animal display to another, Erica couldn't help but admire the patience Caleb exhibited with Hannah. She had a million questions about each animal they saw, and he had a million answers.

It warmed Erica's heart to see the two interact— Hannah and her "Mr. Man." Erica didn't know exactly what was happening with Caleb McMann. She wasn't sure where they were heading or if they were heading anywhere.

All she knew for certain was that she liked Caleb. He was funny and warm, sexy and caring. Being with him felt good and it had been a very long time since Erica had felt confident about life, about what the future held. She only knew for certain that it felt right to be with Caleb. And for now, that was enough.

She only hoped he didn't break Hannah's heart. She only hoped he didn't break her own heart.

"Who's hungry?" she asked as they left the seal pool.

"I am!" Hannah exclaimed.

"I'm so hungry I almost stole one of those little fishies they were feeding the seals," Caleb said.

Peals of laughter escaped Hannah. "Mommy didn't

pack little fishies in the picnic basket, but she did make fried chicken.''

"Mmm, my favorite," Caleb exclaimed. "I'll race you both to the car." Laughing with abandonment, Erica followed after the two.

An hour later Erica and Caleb sat on a blanket beneath a large oak tree, finishing up the last of lunch. Hannah had already eaten and was playing nearby with a couple of other children on the park swings.

"I am stuffed." Caleb groaned and rolled onto his back.

"I would think so after all the chicken you put away," Erica said with a laugh.

"Three pieces."

"Four," she countered.

He grinned at her. "I didn't know you were counting."

"I've got brownies for dessert."

He groaned again. "Not for me."

"Homemade," she said to tempt him.

He laughed. "Really, I couldn't eat another bite." He sat up. "You must have gotten up at the crack of dawn to cook all this stuff."

"I did get up early," she admitted. "I was looking forward to the day." She couldn't very well tell him she'd awakened early with the taste of sweet dreams still on her lips, the vision of him dancing in her head. Her dreams had been of kissing Caleb, of stroking the hard muscles of his body, of his hands touching her, setting her on fire.

"I was looking forward to the day, too." His eyes sparkled with naked desire, as if he'd participated in her dreams and still held the vision in his head.

She held his gaze for a long moment, wondering when he'd become more than a pleasant neighbor, when she'd lost control, abandoned her adamant resolution to keep distance between them.

She broke the gaze as a renewed flood of heat rippled through her. He frightened her because he was making her want him. He made her remember half-forgotten dreams of sharing hopes, of whispered words in the night.

He made her remember all the things she'd once wanted from marriage, all the dreams Chuck and the reality of life had stolen away.

Again she directed her attention toward Hannah. "Her birthday is in two weeks. I'm going to have a big party for her." She looked back at Caleb. "She'd like you to be there."

"What would *you* like?" He studied her intently and she had the feeling he was holding his breath, awaiting her reply.

Her cheeks warmed. "I'd like it, too." She busied herself packing the last of their items in the basket.

"Maybe by then I'll have the tree house completely done."

"That would make a wonderful birthday surprise," Erica said. "I still say you shouldn't have built it. It's an extravagant indulgence for a neighbor's child."

He pulled his knees up toward his chest and

wrapped his arms around them, his expression thoughtful. "I wanted her to have it." His voice held a deep intensity. "Every child should have one extravagant, indulgent dream come true, especially a brave, sweet child like Hannah."

Erica laughed. "A brave, sweet child who is suddenly developing a stubborn streak and a touch of rebellion." She eyed Caleb curiously. "Do you ever think about having children of your own?"

"Sure." His gaze went to Hannah. "When we first got married, Judith and I talked about having half a dozen." He shrugged and looked back at Erica. "But it wasn't meant to be." He cleared his throat, as if his memories had created a lump of emotion he needed to swallow. "What about you? Did you just want one, or did you at one time dream of an entire household of rug rats?"

"Looking back now with hindsight, I think Chuck didn't want children at all. From the time I was small, I wanted lots and lots of babies." She smiled wistfully. "But, like you, I guess it wasn't meant to be."

She set the basket at the side of the blanket. "I also realize now that I was lucky I just had Hannah when Chuck left. I don't think more children would have made him stay. He didn't like being married and with or without Hannah's illness, I don't think we would have made it together. I think maybe I married him for all the wrong reasons."

"Wrong reasons? Like what?"

Erica stretched out on her side and propped herself

up on an elbow. "I was twelve when my father walked away from our family. My mother tried to explain to me and my brother Keith that he wasn't leaving us, just her. But it felt like he left all of us, because we never saw him again."

"I'm sorry," Caleb said softly. "It must have been hard to lose a parent when you were so young." He stretched out on his side, facing her with only a mere foot or so of space between them.

"It was hard," she admitted. "I didn't realize it at the time, but Dad left a void in me that was so deep, so painful. I met Chuck when I was seventeen. He was five years older than me and instantly, he filled the void. I thought it was love at the time, but I realize now it wasn't."

She blushed, realizing she'd been rambling on about personal things she'd never shared with anyone else. "And now you know my whole, boring life story."

"There is nothing I could ever find remotely boring about you or your life," he countered.

Erica blushed again, feeling as if he were seducing her with his gaze, with his words.

At that moment their conversation was interrupted as Hannah came running toward them. "Now can we go see the lions and the tigers?"

"I'll show you a lion." Caleb jumped up and growled as Hannah giggled with delight.

The rest of the afternoon flew by as the three of them continued their exploration of the zoo. Between seeing animals, they ate snow cones and popcorn and chattered nonstop about the wonders of the animal kingdom.

By the time they finally left, darkness was falling and Hannah was exhausted. She buckled herself into the back seat of Caleb's car and promptly fell sound asleep.

"I'd say she had a full day," Caleb said.

"A full day and no nap." Erica smiled at him.

"Yeah, how's the quiet time working out?"

Erica leaned back against the seat and sighed with contentment. "Good. She doesn't sleep, but at least I know she's resting."

"What are you going to do when she starts school? I don't think they provide rest time in first grade."

"She's not going to school," Erica replied.

Caleb looked at her in surprise. "What do you mean?"

"I intend to do just what I did this year. Home schooling."

"Why would you want to do that?" he asked. "I mean, Hannah is such a social butterfly. I'd think she'd thrive on the interaction with other children."

Erica frowned and rubbed her forehead with two fingers. "I don't know...I've been torn about this very subject for the past couple of months. Every day September grows closer, and I'm not sure what the right thing for Hannah is."

"What does she want?"

"To go to public school." Erica drew another deep breath. How could she explain the deep fear that was her constant companion…the fear that fate would once again kick them down, the fear that when things got too good, a fall was inevitable. "But it frightens me so."

Caleb reached his hand out and grabbed hers. "Sooner or later, Erica, you have to let her go."

"I know." She entwined her fingers with his, warmed by the connection, despite the discomfort she felt at the topic of conversation. "It's just that I've been so careful for so long, there have been so many disappointments…unexpected relapses. What if her immune system can't tolerate being around so many children? What if her heart can't take the stress, the excitement of school?"

"What does her doctor say?"

"He thinks she's ready to run marathons, race the wind or whatever else she has in mind."

"Nobody has the final decision but you." He squeezed her hand. "I just worry about you."

"About me?" She looked at him in surprise.

"You can't be all and everything to her, Erica. As much as you love her, as much as you want to protect her, you have to build something of your own, something separate from your child. When you build your life around a child, and then that child goes away, you're left with nothing to hang on to, no reason to go on."

His voice held an intensity that startled her. Was he talking about his experience with his wife? Had he built his world around her, only to lose her to a tragic illness? Had he been left with nothing to hang on to but desolation? Regrets? Loneliness?

He was telling her the same things Sherry had told her a million times before, but they sounded different coming from Caleb. Erica knew he spoke from common experience, understood the fear of loss.

"Home again, home again," he said as he pulled into her driveway.

"Jiggety-jig." She smiled at him, feeling closer to him than she had at any time before.

"I'll help you get sleeping beauty tucked in," he said as they got out of the car.

It took him only minutes to pick up the sleeping child and carry her into the house and to bed. She didn't stir as Erica took off her shoes, and changed her into her pajamas. Erica softly kissed her cheek, then pulled the sheet up around her.

As Erica left the room, Caleb draped an arm across her shoulders. "This has been another wonderful day," he said as they walked back to the living room.

"Yes, it has been." She stopped walking and faced him, conscious of the energized air between them. She'd felt it all day, a simmering sexual tension on the verge of exploding. She'd been acutely aware of each inadvertent touch between them, every brush of shoulder or bump of thigh.

"Would you like to stay for coffee?" she asked.

He reached out and touched her cheek, then trailed a finger across her bottom lip. His touch shot sparks of heat through her. "I don't think that would be a good idea. I don't think I'd be satisfied with just coffee.''

His gaze set her aflame. ''I have some cookies,'' she whispered in an attempt at humor. But his eyes held a hunger that stole her breath away and set her heart pounding.

''Even cookies wouldn't satisfy me tonight.'' He pulled her into his arms and claimed her lips with his. His mouth moved over hers with fiery intensity, and Erica responded with the hunger that had been building inside her since the moment she'd first met him.

She wound her arms around his neck and molded herself to him, wanting to feel him as intimately close to her as possible. He groaned and tangled his hands in her hair as his mouth left hers and instead trailed hot kisses down the side of her neck, along the hollow of her throat.

Erica's head spun dizzily as the sweet rush of desire swept through her. She wanted him. She wanted him to touch her, wanted him to stroke her body. And she wanted to do the same to him. She wanted to run her hands across his chest, taste his skin. She wanted to make love with him.

More than anything, she wanted to wake up in his arms, see him in that first blush of morning. But that wasn't going to happen. She had a daughter to consider, and there was no way she could allow Caleb to spend the night here and confuse Hannah.

His hands moved from the length of her hair down

to the small of her back, then cupped her buttocks and pulled her tight against him.

She could feel his desire...hard and unyielding against her pelvis. At the same time his mouth once again covered hers.

Control was slipping away, and Erica knew she had to call a halt or else she would be lost. "Caleb..." She placed her hands on his shoulders and gently pushed at him.

Instantly he dropped his hands and stepped back from her, although his eyes still radiated the depth of his desire. "Sorry, I didn't mean anything but a simple kiss."

She smiled, her cheeks warm with pleasure. "Kissing you, Caleb, is anything but simple."

He returned her smile, his gaze impossibly warm on her. "If you keep looking at me like that, I swear I'll have no choice but to kiss you again." He took another step away from her. "I'd better just say goodnight."

"Maybe that would be best," she agreed softly, although she heard the wistful longing in her own voice. "Good night, Caleb."

She locked the door after him, her heart still beating rapidly. Her breasts ached, her legs felt weak, her entire body screamed with the need to be loved.... Her desire had a name, and its name was Caleb.

However, beneath the ache, beyond the desire, was a touch of fear. He was too good to be true. Granted, it was obvious that he wanted her, but he hadn't even decided if he was staying in St. Louis or not.

He'd made no promises to her, whispered no words of love. He'd just looked at her with desire in his eyes, a desire that could burn out as quickly as it had fanned into flames.

She couldn't chance it. She couldn't stand to be hurt again and she steadfastly refused to consider allowing Hannah's fragile heart to be hurt by any man.

Despite all the reasons why she shouldn't see Caleb again, why she knew she should withdraw from him, protect her heart and Hannah's, as she got into bed moments later, she wondered when she'd see him again. When she could taste his lips once more.

It was absolutely crazy, and something she'd always maintained would never happen...but she just might be falling in love again.

Chapter 8

Faces swirled before him. Katie's face...Hannah's, Judith's and Erica's. Each of them spoke to him, but he couldn't hear the words they were saying. He strained, trying to make sense out of the jumble of voices.

He laughed with joy as he discerned Katie's voice amid the confusion. "I love you, Daddy Doodle," she said, then laughed that special, little-girl laugh that so warmed his heart.

I love you, Caleb wanted to say. I love you, Katie, and you'll always be in my heart. Before he could say the words aloud, a foghorn blew and the four female faces disappeared into the ocean.

The foghorn blew again, transforming itself into the ring of the telephone. Caleb sat up and grabbed for the phone near the bed, his mind still muddled with his crazy dream.

"Caleb McMann, what in the hell are you doing?" His sister Sarah's voice boomed over the line.

He rubbed a hand across his jaw, trying to reenter the world of reality and leave his dreamscape behind. "I was sleeping. It's nice to hear your sweet voice," he said with more than a touch of sarcasm.

"Sleeping? It's after nine."

Caleb looked at the clock on the bedside table. Indeed, it was almost nine-thirty. "I was up most of the night finishing a project, so I decided to sleep in this morning."

"Caleb, what in the hell are you doing?" she repeated. This time her voice was softer, beseeching. "Why aren't you back in Chicago where you belong? What's happening with your business? You're letting everything go to hell."

"Nonsense," he scoffed. "My business is doing fine. I'm in daily touch with my foremen by telephone and fax."

"I'm so worried about you. You need to come home."

"I can't go back yet." Caleb frowned and raked a hand through his hair. "I haven't had enough time...I need to be here."

"You need to be home in Chicago, getting on with your life," she countered. "You can't turn that little girl into Katie. Katie is gone."

"I know that," Caleb said with a touch of irritation.

"I'm not trying to make her into Katie." He drew a deep sigh. "All I know is that I need to be here, that it's right that I'm here. I can't explain it, Sarah, but this is where I'm supposed to be right now. I know it in my heart. I know it in my soul."

His words were met with silence, then Sarah sighed. "How do I argue with that?"

Caleb laughed. "You don't."

"Are you sure you're okay?" Her worry was evident in her tone. "You want me to come out there? I have a little vacation time coming."

"Please. That isn't necessary. Sarah, I promise I'm fine," he assured her.

"When you told me you were going out there, I thought you meant for a weekend, a week at the most. But, Caleb, it's been a month."

"I know."

"And you're sure you know what you're doing?"

He laughed again. "No, I wouldn't go that far."

They chatted for a minute or two longer, then hung up. Caleb got out of bed and pulled on a pair of jeans, then padded down the stairs to the kitchen. He poured himself a cup of coffee, then moved to the window that looked out onto his backyard and beyond it, into Erica's backyard.

She and Hannah were out there, stringing crepe paper and other decorations for the birthday party that would begin at eleven. He knew if he cracked open his window, he'd probably be able to hear their laughter as they prepared for the momentous occasion.

Caleb had worked through the night to finish the tree house, which was now covered with half a dozen drop cloths, effectively hiding the structure from view.

A smile touched his lips as he imagined Hannah's reaction when he unveiled it. He knew she would be delighted. It had turned out magnificently, better than even he had imagined.

The tree house wasn't the only gift he had for her. He'd also bought a doll. She was a beauty, with long golden curls and big blue eyes, a hand-painted porcelain face and a number on her foot that proclaimed her a collectible.

What in the hell are you doing? Sarah's words replayed in his mind. Yes, what in the hell *was* he doing? The past two weeks had gone by like a dream. He'd worked on the house, conducted his construction business by phone, and shared every spare minute he had with Erica and Hannah.

They'd gone out for pizza, seen a movie, and enjoyed another trip to the zoo. They'd talked, and laughed, and he and Erica had sneaked furtive kisses whenever the opportunity presented itself. The only thing he hadn't done was told her the truth.

He told himself he was waiting for the perfect time to tell her, but he knew the real truth. Fear kept him silent. A fear that lived with him each day and every night. He turned away from the window with a frown.

He wasn't going to think about it today. It was a day of celebration. Hannah Marie Clemmons's sixth birthday. The sixth birthday for a little girl the doctors had thought might not see her first. Yes, it was a day for joy, not for confessions.

He thought about going over to help them decorate, but decided to allow them that pleasure alone. It seemed right that mother and daughter prepare for the day without the intrusion of a neighbor.

A neighbor. He knew he'd become more than that to Erica. Her laughter, the warmth of her gaze on him, the heat of her mouth when they kissed—all these things told him that.

And she had certainly become more than a neighbor to him. She'd become far more than just the mother of a child he wanted to connect with. *What in the hell are you doing, Caleb?* He honestly didn't know.

He puttered around the house until ten-thirty, then showered and dressed for the party. As he left the house, the sun bore down on him, letting him know it was going to be a brutally hot day.

"Mr. Man!" Hannah greeted him as he came through the gate that separated the two yards. "It's a happy birthday day!"

"Indeed it is," he replied. He held out the gift he carried. "I don't suppose you know who this pretty present might be for?"

"For me!" She took the present and jumped up and down. "Come on. Mommy is inside getting stuff ready to cook on the barbecue."

Caleb followed Hannah through the back door and into the cool interior of the kitchen. Thank goodness he'd made certain they had central air before it got so warm.

Erica stood at the counter slicing tomatoes. Clad in a turquoise-colored backless sundress and wearing her hair braided into a single strand down her back, she momentarily stole Caleb's breath away with her beauty.

"Hi," he said. "Anything I can do to help?"

"Sure. While I'm slicing the tomatoes, you can peel the carrots for a relish tray." She handed him a vegetable peeler and a bag of carrots.

"What can I do, Mommy?" Hannah asked, obviously eager to take part in the preparations.

"Why don't you set out the napkins and the cutlery on the picnic table outside," Erica suggested.

"Okay." Hannah grabbed the boxes of plastic utensils and the package of gaily decorated napkins, then skipped out the back door.

The moment she disappeared from sight, Caleb took Erica by the shoulders and spun her around to face him. "How's the mother of the birthday girl doing?"

Her cheeks were flushed and her eyes sparkled with pleasure. "It's a wonderful day for a celebration, Caleb. I feel magnificent."

"You look more than magnificent," he said, wondering if he'd ever tire of looking at her. He couldn't imagine not wanting to gaze into the luminous blue of her eyes, or to watch the expressions on her lovely face.

"You don't look so bad yourself." Her eyes, a perfect match for the turquoise dress, flirted with him and her lips, pink and shiny, beckoned him. His heart raced as he dipped his head to kiss her.

He'd intended a light, playful kiss, but the instant his mouth met hers, his desire for her raged nearly out of control.

Greedily, he took possession of her lips, knowing he would never be satisfied until he had the experience of making love to her. And he sensed the hunger in her...the hunger for him, and that only stoked the flames of his desire.

The doorbell pealed, a jarring sound that effectively doused the fire raging between them. They sprang apart like guilty teenagers caught in the act by their parents.

"Saved by the bell," he whispered, his words rewarded by her musical giggle.

In the next fifteen minutes, the house quickly filled with people. Sherry and her husband, David, were the first to arrive, quickly followed by Erica's brother Keith, his wife, Amy, and their three children.

Caleb took change of the barbecue grill, preparing the charcoal and setting it alight. As the flames died down and the charcoal turned gray, Keith approached him with a friendly smile.

"Erica was just telling me you've accomplished wonders in that house of yours," he said.

Caleb nodded. "Yeah, I'm pretty pleased with the results. Other than a little bit of finish work, the place looks like new."

"You intending to sell?"

"Haven't decided yet." Caleb smiled at Keith. "I like this neighborhood. I've grown especially fond of a couple of my neighbors."

Keith looked over to where his sister was chatting with Amy and Sherry. "You've been good for her," he said softly.

"She's been good for me," Caleb countered.

"No, you don't understand. When Erica's husband left her and Hannah was so sick, Erica shut herself off from everyone, including me and Amy. She crawled so far inside her shell nobody could reach her except Hannah." Keith smiled and looked back at Caleb. "But, I see her opening again. Finally, after all these years, I see hope in her eyes. If it's at all possible, try not to hurt her."

Caleb looked at him in surprise. "I have no intention of hurting her." He frowned, ignoring the bell of guilt that rang in his head. He prayed that when he finally told her the truth, it wouldn't cause her any pain.

"Good. Erica is the only family I have and I care about her a lot, although she doesn't seem to realize that."

"Oh, I'm sure she knows," Caleb protested.

Keith frowned thoughtfully. "I wish I could be sure. We weren't real close when we were growing up. She was only twelve when I left home for the army. She was mad at me when I left, and I don't think she ever really forgave me."

He shrugged, a light flush stealing over his features. "And how about that kid?" Keith gestured toward Hannah, who was chasing one of her cousins, her hair flying wildly as her giggles filled the air. "God, I can't believe how great she looks, how completely healthy."

"She's a special little girl," Caleb said.

"Yes, she is, and that's why I keep nagging Erica to share her with her cousins. It's important to me that Hannah and my children are close. Kids need family."

"I agree," Caleb replied.

"Good." Keith offered him another smile and Caleb had the feeling the conversation was more than just idle talk.

"How's the charcoal?" Erica called as Keith wandered off.

"Ready to cook on," Caleb returned.

"Looks hot," she observed as she approached.

"Why, thank you, ma'am," Caleb said teasingly. "I was hoping you'd think I looked hot when I put on these shorts."

She laughed and nudged him in the ribs. "You're terrible," she exclaimed. "Just for that, you get to cook all the hamburgers."

The afternoon flew by. They ate hamburgers and hot dogs, played games with the kids, ate cake and ice cream and sang "Happy Birthday" to Hannah.

It was nearly four when Hannah started to open her presents. She exclaimed in delight over the game from her cousins, squealed happily as she unwrapped a pup tent and plastic flashlight and canteen from Sherry and David.

At that moment Caleb knew he'd made a mistake. The doll had been a terrible mistake. Clarity rang through his mind and he realized he'd bought the doll for Katie, who loved ruffles and frills, and tea parties and dolls.

But, Katie was dead. And despite the fact that Katie's heart now pumped in Hannah's chest, Hannah wasn't Katie, would never be Katie.

Grief seared through him. Raw grief that momentarily stole his breath away. Despite the technology that could place the heart of one child into the chest of another, nothing would miraculously bring back his child. Katie was gone, and the doll was wrong…all wrong for Hannah.

Hannah opened the present and smiled politely. "Thank you, Mr. Man. She's very pretty."

"She is pretty," Caleb agreed. "But I don't think she's right for you. How about tomorrow you and I go back to the store, return the doll and then you can pick out something you really want."

Hannah looked at her mother, who hesitated a moment then gave a subtle nod. "Okay," Hannah agreed happily. "Maybe I can trade her in for a baseball mitt."

Caleb smiled and nodded, his heart still aching with residual emotion. From tea parties to baseball mitts, it was time to say goodbye to the little girl who had once been his. He would always grieve for her, but his grief was finding a place in his heart that didn't hurt quite as much, quite as often as it had.

"And now, it's time to unveil my real birthday present," Caleb said. "Why don't we move the party to my backyard for a few minutes?"

Soon the party had congregated beneath the hidden tree house. "Let me see, let me see," Hannah exclaimed, jumping up and down with excitement. "I know it's going to be the bestest tree house in the whole, wide world."

"Okay," Caleb laughed. He climbed up the stairs and quickly removed the drop cloths, revealing the structure beneath. Painted white, with two small windows complete with pink curtains, the tree house was every child's dream. But Hannah's name was carefully painted above the small doorway, proclaiming it her dream alone.

There was a moment of stunned silence. "Oh, Mr. Man, it's so perfect." Hannah threw herself into his arms and hugged him tight. "I knew it. I knew it would be the bestest in the world, and it is."

Caleb closed his eyes and hugged her back. This time, as he smelled the sweet child scent of her, felt her snuggly warmth, there was no confusion in his mind. This was Hannah, not Katie.

And although a piece of his heart would always belong to the child he had lost, there was still enough left to love Hannah as well.

He released Hannah and watched as she and her cousins scampered up the stairs to the tree house. He realized that in the space of the last few minutes, a profound healing had taken place in his heart. For the first time since Katie's death, he realized he could survive, that he was truly going to be all right.

Erica watched her daughter playing in the tree house with her cousins, her heart soaring with every giggle that resonated in the air. There was no sound sweeter in the world than that of children laughing, and she couldn't remember a time when Hannah had had so much fun.

She looked over at Caleb, who was visiting with Sherry's husband. He looked tremendously good in his navy walking shorts and short-sleeved shirt. He caught her gaze and smiled at her, a smile that weakened her knees and sent a rivulet of heat through her.

"Great party, Erica."

She turned and smiled at her brother. "It's been a perfect day."

Keith looked over toward the tree house, then back at her. "It's good to see them all together. They're terrific together."

"Yes, they are," she agreed.

"Why don't you let Hannah come home with us, spend the night? We could have her back here at whatever time you decide in the morning."

Tension exploded inside Erica's stomach. Spend the night? A night when Hannah would not be safely beneath Erica's roof? A flutter of familiar fear washed over her. "Oh, Keith, I don't think…"

"Let us share in her life," Keith interrupted. He placed a hand on Erica's arm. "Please, Erica. I can't tell you what it would mean to me and Amy and our kids if we could be a real, close family."

She hesitated, torn between her fear and her love for both her brother and her child. "It's already been such a big day for Hannah. Why don't I let her go home with you just for the evening? I'll pick her up around ten and we'll plan an overnight visit for another time."

Keith opened his mouth as if to protest, then apparently thought better of it and merely nodded. "Okay," he agreed.

Erica reached out and gave him a quick hug. "It's a start, right?"

He laughed. "Yeah, it's a start."

By six, the party was winding down. Sherry and David said their goodbyes and left, and Amy and Keith and their brood, plus one, quickly followed.

"I'll help with the cleanup," Caleb said as he pulled down strands of crepe paper and wadded them up.

"You don't have to do that," Erica protested half-heartedly, then flashed him a smile. "But it's nice of you to offer."

His answering smile once again sent rivers of warmth flooding through her, warmth that intensified as she realized they had the house to themselves.

Hannah was gone for the evening, and if Caleb decided to kiss her, there would be no real reason for him to stop for a very long time.

She carefully focused her attention on putting the last of the leftovers away in the refrigerator and tried not to think about the potential of an empty house and Caleb.

Thirty minutes later both the kitchen and the backyard were back to normal. All the extra food had been dealt with and the trash had been bagged away.

"How about a tall glass of lemonade?" she asked Caleb, feeling ridiculously nervous as he stood by the table and gazed at her.

"No, I don't think so." He took several steps toward her.

Erica swallowed, realizing her mouth was achingly dry. "Coffee?"

His eyes glittered darkly. "No, thanks." Two more steps. He now stood close enough to her that she could see the silver flecks in his eyes, feel the body heat that radiated from him.

"Then...what would you like?" she asked breathlessly.

"You."

The word sizzled through her and if he hadn't reached for her at that moment, she would have thrown herself at him.

Their mouths met in fiery splendor as the tension that had been building between them for the last month exploded in a volcano of emotion.

His mouth was hot...hot enough to light a fire inside her, and when he finally broke the kiss, she took him by the hand and led him through the living room toward her bedroom.

As they walked, her heart beat out a thunderous rhythm. She knew they were about to cross the final boundary, become more than neighbors, more than friends.

He'd made no promises to her, spoken no flowery words of love, but at the moment that didn't matter. She wanted him, with or without a commitment of any kind. This was her choice, and she didn't care about tomorrow or forever...just tonight...with Caleb.

She recognized exactly what she was doing; her mind wasn't addled by party gaiety or fogged by desire. She wanted to feel Caleb's hands on her, his lips on her. She wanted to touch him and feel his body take possession of hers...even if it was just for a night.

Her bedroom was lit with the dusty gold of fading twilight and shadows danced on the walls as night moved to steal the last of the day. When they entered the room, he released her hand and took a step back, his eyes sparkling pools of desire.

"Are you sure?" he asked, his voice deep and husky. "I want you so badly I ache with it. For the last couple of weeks I haven't been able to think of anything else. But I want you to be sure...I don't want you to think this was a mistake in the light of tomorrow."

When he was finished, Erica didn't say a word. Instead, she reached up behind her neck and untied the halter top of her dress, then allowed it to drop to her waist, exposing her naked breasts. He had his answer.

In two long strides, he had her once again in his embrace, his mouth moving hungrily over hers. Her breasts were pressed tight against the fabric of his shirt, but she didn't want contact with the material. She wanted to feel his chest, his firm, warm skin intimately close to hers.

With her mouth still connected to his, she moved her hands up to unfasten the shirt buttons. Her fingers fumbled and tripped over themselves in her eagerness to undress him.

He laughed, a low, sexy chuckle, and helped her with last of the buttons, then tore the shirt off and tossed it to the floor.

His hands worked to unbraid her hair and loosen it from its confines. Once it was freed, he wrapped his fingers into it, tugging her head backward so his mouth could press against the throbbing pulse point at the base of her throat.

Then, with slow, but purposeful movements, his fingers unwound from her hair and moved to the zipper at her waist. When he unzipped it, the dress released itself from her and fell into a turquoise pool at her feet.

Someplace in the back of her mind, she was grateful that she'd worn her lacy briefs instead of the sturdy white cotton ones. Gently, he walked her to the bed and eased her down on the rose-colored spread, then stepped back, his eyes intently holding hers, before trailing down the length of her.

As his gaze touched her intimately, she felt no need to cover her near-nakedness, no self-consciousness whatsoever. She saw in his eyes that he thought she was beautiful, sensed his desire in the tension of his body.

She opened her arms, beckoning him to join her. He took off his walking shorts, revealing a pair of black briefs that emphasized his slender waist, slim hips and his urgent need of her.

He joined her on the bed and they tangled together as their mouths once again sought each other's. His kiss was demanding, greedy, and Erica met it with a deep hunger of her own. She felt as if she could kiss him for an eternity and even that wouldn't be long enough.

When he finally broke the kiss and lowered his head, his mouth finding the taut peak of one breast, she cried out in wonder.

Had it been this magnificent before? Had Chuck's touch ever moved her to such heights? No...never in her life had she experienced the kind of liquid fire Caleb's touch stoked in her veins.

As Caleb continued to kiss her breasts, his tongue flicking teasingly across the tender tips, Erica ran her hands down his glorious back, reveling in the play of strong muscle beneath warm skin.

Her fingernails dug into his back as his hands left her breasts and instead trailed down her ribs, across the expanse of her abdomen and lingered at the low-cut band of her panties.

She didn't want his hesitation, didn't want him to tease her. She moved her hips provocatively, felt his swift intake of breath, then his fingers were on her, caressing her through the thin silk.

Closing her eyes, she gave herself over to the sweet sensations that coursed through her. Then his fingers were no longer on the silk, but beneath it; then the panties were gone altogether and the tension inside her climbed higher and higher. She felt her release approaching and stopped moving, wanting...needing him to go there with her.

She opened her eyes and spoke his name, a whisper of yearning. He groaned in reply and rolled on top of her. She vaguely realized that at some point he'd removed his briefs.

His lips took possession of hers at the same time he entered her. For a long moment neither of them moved, as if afraid a single motion would instantly carry them over the edge.

He raised up slightly and looked at her, then raked a finger across her lower lip. "I'm sorry. I want this to last forever, but I'm afraid it's going to be too fast...."

She touched his cheek and nodded, then lost herself in him as he moved his hips against hers, taking complete possession of her body, her heart, her soul.

Caleb couldn't get enough of her, but knew the long-suffering anticipation coupled with the reality of making love to Erica would make the entire act pass far too quickly.

He tried to maintain control, tried desperately to make each moment, every sensation last as long as possible. But her mouth tasted too sweet, her body accepted his with such evocative warmth, and he felt all restraint slipping away.

Not yet, his mind pleaded, not wanting it to end, wanting to take her with him to the highest peak of pleasure. Faster and faster they moved together, and he felt her tension rising...building...and when his release came, she cried out his name as he carried her with him over the edge.

For a long moment they remained entwined, their bodies covered with a light sheen of sweat as their heartbeats slowed to a more normal rhythm.

"You okay?" he finally asked her. They untangled and he propped himself up on one arm so he could look at her. Her cheeks were flushed, her lips slightly swollen, and she'd never looked more lovely to Caleb.

She smiled, her eyelids fluttering with drowsiness. "I can't remember the last time I felt this okay." She snuggled against him, her breath warm against the hollow of his throat.

Caleb rubbed his hand down the length of her slender back and a fierce protectiveness surged through him. A few minutes later, a wave of tenderness followed as he realized she'd fallen asleep.

She'd probably been up at the crack of dawn preparing for the party. It had been a big day for her...for Hannah...and for him.

He thought of that moment when Hannah had opened his present, when he'd realized for the first time that he'd somehow been searching for pieces of Katie in Hannah...for pieces that weren't there.

Katie's heart had given Hannah life, but it hadn't given Hannah memories of Caleb. Although the realization that his little girl was gone forever hurt, there was also a calming sense of peace in the knowledge that he didn't have to search any further than his own heart for the loving memories he needed to sustain him.

But at the moment his mind was not filled with memories of Katie; it was full of Erica. Making love to Erica had been better than his best dream. Her touch excited him, her beauty humbled him, and her abandoned passion had stirred him to heights he'd never reached before.

Even now, thinking about what they had just shared caused his blood to heat and made him feel as if he were capable of making love to her all over again. He threw an arm across his forehead, enjoying the snuggly warmth of Erica's body against his.

Then, all at once, a cold wind of guilt blew through him.

What in the hell was he doing?

How could he make love to Erica, hold her in his arms, and still keep the secret that burned in his heart? What kind of a man was he?

Yet even as the questions unfolded in his mind, he knew the answers. He hadn't told her about Katie and Hannah yet because he knew it would destroy the fragile, but miraculous relationship that was building between them. He hadn't told her yet because he knew she would send him away...and he was falling in love with her.

And he didn't know what in the hell to do about that.

Chapter 9

Caleb sat on his back porch, watching Hannah play in the tree house. A little while before she had carried half a dozen stuffed animals up the stairs, explaining to Caleb that they were her baseball team and she was going to coach them for the big game.

From his vantage point he could see Erica sitting at the picnic table in her backyard working on a laptop computer. He knew she was working on a newsletter she wanted to get out by the next day.

Although there was nothing he'd like more than to go over and join her, he didn't want to make a nuisance of himself while she was working.

She was sitting outside because Stanley had a crew of men painting the interior of the house. She didn't know Stanley's attentiveness was thanks to a healthy

check Caleb had written for the work. The day her
central-air unit had been installed, he'd watched her
dance happily throughout the rooms, marveling that
the entire place was wonderfully pleasant in temperature.

He sipped a glass of iced tea, enjoying the cooler
temperature an overnight shower had brought. July
was half gone and August was just around the corner.
It was hard to believe that he'd been in St. Louis for
over five weeks.

It had been a week since Hannah's birthday party,
since the night he'd held Erica in his arms, tasted the
sweetness of her lips, enjoyed the pleasure of making
love to her.

Throughout the past seven days, the three of them
had spent a lot of time together. They had gone to the
movies, seen a ball game and spent the rest of the
evenings sitting on her back porch watching Hannah
play. Idyllic times…the stuff of dreams.

Every minute of every one of those seven days,
Caleb had wanted to make love to Erica again, but the
opportunity hadn't presented itself. Even without making love to her, the depths of his feelings for her had
grown daily. What had begun as a quest to get to know
Hannah had ended with him falling in love with Hannah's mother.

What filled him with abounding joy was the knowledge that Erica was falling in love with him as well.
Although she hadn't expressed her growing feelings
for him in words, each gesture, every glance spoke

eloquently of her deepening emotions where he was concerned.

He frowned and took another sip of his iced tea. Someplace in the back of his mind, he knew what he was doing. He was hoping if he waited long enough, if he gave her more time, she would love him too deeply to send him away when he finally told her the truth about who he was and what had brought him to St. Louis. He was gambling...and knew it was the most important gamble of his entire life.

Loving Erica had filled him with a new sense of hope, opened the door to old dreams and new possibilities, unleashed a renewed fervor for life, one that had been previously stolen from him by tragedy.

"Mr. Man." Hannah peeked out the door of her tree house.

"What, munchkin?" He smiled up at her.

"If I play baseball on a real team, would you teach me how to catch real good?"

"Sure," he agreed easily. "And I'll teach you how to pitch, too."

"Oh boy! Thanks, Mr. Man." She disappeared once again into the little house.

He smiled to himself. Definitely not Katie. The last thing Katie would have ever wanted to do was join a baseball team. Katie would have preferred to stand on the sidelines at a game wearing a cheerleader outfit with matching ribbons in her hair.

Two very separate little girls. Both special, and both

owning a piece of his heart. But, never again would he confuse the two.

"I love you, Daddy Doodle." If he closed his eyes and listened real hard, he could hear Katie's sweet, childish voice. She would always be with him in spirit. The peace his thoughts brought him let him know his healing continued.

He heard Erica's phone ring and watched as she picked up the cordless by her side.

Erica.

He loved her.

He loved the way she tucked her hair behind her ear as she thought. He loved the way her eyes lit with laughter first, before it reached her lips. He loved everything about her and it filled him with the kind of happiness he'd thought he'd never find again.

He stood as he saw Erica approaching. As she came through the gate into his yard, she flashed him a smile, although he sensed tension in her body.

"Everything all right?" he asked, fighting the impulse to touch her, pull her into his arms.

She nodded. "Hannah?" she yelled up the ladder to the tree house.

Hannah reappeared in the doorway. "Hi, Mommy. Wanna come up and visit?"

"No thanks, sweetie. I was wondering if you'd like to spend the night with Aunt Amy and Uncle Keith and Mary, Samantha and little Billy?"

"For real?" Hannah's face lit up with excitement.

"And I could spend the whole night, and wake up there in the morning?"

"The whole night," Erica agreed. Although she smiled at Hannah, Caleb could see the shadows of doubt, of fear that darkened her eyes.

"Oh, boy!" Hannah scampered down the ladder and threw her arms around her mother's waist. "When can I go?"

"As soon as you pack an overnight bag with your pajamas and toothbrush."

Before the entire sentence was out of Erica's mouth, Hannah was racing for the house to prepare the bag.

Caleb laughed. "I think she's a little excited."

Erica nodded. "I wish I were."

Caleb wrapped an arm around her and pulled her close. "She'll be fine," he assured her.

She smiled up at him. "Intellectually, I know that. I know this is right. It's time I let her go, and Keith will take good care of her. But, emotionally, it's a little bit frightening. A whole night away from me."

"But it's the best thing." He squeezed her close, as always half-intoxicated by her nearness.

She nodded. "I know it is." She moved out of his embrace. "I'd better go help her pack." She started to leave.

"Erica?"

She turned back to look at him.

"While Hannah is at your brother's house playing childish games, why don't you come over here for supper about seven and I'll teach you some grown-up games.''

Her eyes flashed her pleasure at his suggestion. ''I'd like that,'' she said softly, then turned and ran back to her own home.

Caleb watched her go, his mind already whirling with thoughts of the evening to come. He'd do a candlelight dinner, complete with good wine and soft music. They could spend time talking, sharing...then make love.

And tonight...he would tell her the truth.

''She'll be fine,'' Keith assured Erica as they walked toward the front door.

''I know,'' Erica replied.

Within minutes of arriving, the three girls had become happily involved in a game of Candy Land. Their girlish giggles filled the house, along with the scent of the popcorn Amy had made for a snack.

''Hannah, want to give me a kiss goodbye?'' Erica called from the door.

''I'll kiss you double tomorrow,'' Hannah replied, obviously not wanting to leave the game for a moment.

''She'll be fine,'' Keith repeated. ''We'll have her home around ten tomorrow. Is that all right?''

''Sure.'' For a moment Erica felt lost.

Keith touched her arm lightly. ''Thanks, Erica. I can't tell you what this means to me and Amy.''

Erica nodded, said her goodbyes, then left. Moments later she was driving home, her thoughts on her daughter. Was it possible to hope? Was the future a shining promise rather than an unknown agony?

Hannah's heart was working better than any of the doctors had dreamed. It appeared that her health problems were finally, irrevocably behind her, but could Erica trust in that? Oh, how she wanted to believe that Hannah would now be able to live a normal, happy life. It was all Erica had ever wanted in life.

Not quite, a small voice whispered in the back of her head. At one time, Erica had entertained other hopes, other dreams. With Hannah's apparent good health, those nebulous fantasies she'd pushed aside for so many years were now re-emerging.

However, Erica knew it wasn't just Hannah's well-being that had evoked the stir of old longings. It was Caleb. His name made her heart soar. He'd given her back her hope. He'd made her realize that not all men ran when the going got tough. Some men stayed, and loved forever.

She looked at her watch as she pulled into her driveway. She had an hour before she was supposed to go over to Caleb's for dinner. Heat suffused her.

Dinner. He'd made it clear that his offer had been for far more than a meal and her heart sang with the knowledge that tonight she'd once again be held in Caleb's arms, taste his lips against hers, feel his body moving intimately against hers.

It wasn't just the thought of making love to him that filled her heart to bursting. It was the connection she felt spiritually when he held her, when he touched her. Desire was one thing…but what she felt for Caleb McMann was far more than just desire.

She pulled into her driveway, her thoughts skipping from Caleb back to Hannah. This would be the first time she and Hannah were apart for an entire night. All those nights in the hospital when Hannah had been so ill, Erica had always slept on a cot or in the chair nearby.

It was the natural order of things that children grew away from their parents, developed identities and personalities that were quite separate. Physically, Hannah was healthy, but in order to encourage her mental and emotional healthiness, Erica had to give her daughter the freedom to grow.

Tiny wings. Hannah was developing tiny wings that would carry her toward the kind of independence that would eventually make her an autonomous, well-adjusted young lady. Yes, the process had already begun, and Erica felt both a bittersweet wistfulness and a fierce pride in Hannah's growth.

She wondered if she'd be so complacent about Hannah's new independence if she didn't have Caleb in her life. If she'd been truly alone, would Hannah's natural development away from her be more frightening?

Thoughts of Caleb once again sent a rush of heat through her. She turned off the car engine and hurried inside the house, wanting time for a long soak in a bubble bath before she met him for dinner…and whatever else the night promised.

An hour later she stood on Caleb's front porch, nervously fiddling with her purse strap. Ridiculous to feel nervous, she chided herself. She hadn't felt nervous around Caleb since the first night they'd gone to the movies together.

He opened the front door, the sparkle in his eyes a perfect foil for the white shirt neatly tucked into a pair of black denims. Dark wisps of chest hair peeked out of the open collar and taunted her with the desire to tangle her fingers into it. "Hi," she said.

"Hi yourself," he returned. He leaned down and kissed the side of her neck, a lingering kiss that inflamed every nerve in her body. "Mmm, you smell like a luscious, ripe strawberry," he said as he ushered her inside.

She laughed. "I used Hannah's strawberry bubble bath." Her breath caught in her throat as she looked around. She hadn't been in the house since he'd done all the work.

There was no furniture in the living room to detract from the gleaming oak floors and trim. The fireplace had been cleaned and the stones glistened with their natural beauty. "Oh Caleb," she said softly. "It's so beautiful."

"It turned out nice, didn't it?" There was no mistaking the pride in his voice. "I've got an appointment tomorrow to talk to somebody about carpeting for this room."

"Oh no!" She blushed apologetically. "Sorry."

"No need to be." He looked around the room, then back at her. "You don't think I should carpet?"

"I think it would be a sin to cover this glorious floor. Maybe a couple of area rugs," she suggested.

His gaze lingered on her thoughtfully. "You're right. Come on, let me show you the rest of the place."

She followed him into the dining room, then the kitchen with its new, gleaming cabinets. "Everything looks just as I always imagined it would...even better."

She gazed at him in admiration. "I used to stand at my kitchen sink and fantasize how this place would look with a little love and attention. You've managed to far exceed my fantasies."

He smiled and held out a hand to her. "Let me show you the upstairs."

His hand was warm and firm around hers, and she liked the way it felt for them to be climbing the stairs side by side. It was far too easy to allow her imagination to take flight, to imagine that they were going up to their bedroom together at the end of a day of shared married life.

Slow down, girl, she cautioned herself. Just because she knew what was in her own heart where Caleb was concerned, didn't mean he felt the same way about her.

Oh, she had no doubt about his desire for her...but

desire was very different from love and the kind of life commitment Erica yearned for.

He led her first into a large, airy bedroom obviously meant as a guest room. Again, there was no furniture in the room, but the paint was fresh, a sun-kissed yellow that gave the room a cheerful personality despite the lack of furnishings.

The next room was the master suite. A bed and dresser let her know this was the room where Caleb slept. She would have known the space as his in any case, for it smelled of him…the pleasant scent of clean male and refreshing cologne.

The bed was neatly made with a navy spread and she could smell the faint scent of lemon polish, as if he'd cleaned the room moments before she'd arrived. The adjoining bathroom also held the same fresh scent and clean navy towels hung on the holder.

"Nice," she said, wondering if he'd cleaned because he knew sooner or later in the evening they would be in this room, in his bed, making love.

"This is my real masterpiece," he said as he led her out of the master suite and into the room across the hall.

Erica clapped her hands together in delight as she walked into the bedroom that was specifically designed with a child in mind.

She ran her hand along the railing of the bunk bed, touched the golden wood of the window seat. The window provided a perfect view of the tree house and it was easy to imagine Hannah spending her quiet time sitting there reading a favorite book.

"Hannah would love a room like this," she said softly, wondering if she would ever be able to provide something similar for her daughter. She turned to look at Caleb once again. "It's wonderful, Caleb. Truly wonderful. You should be able to sell the place with no problem whatsoever."

"Yeah. If that's what I eventually decide to do. We'd better go downstairs and let me check on our dinner."

If that's what I eventually decide to do. His words echoed in Erica's mind with promise as they went back downstairs to the kitchen. So he hasn't made up his mind yet, she thought. Maybe he'll stay. Please, please...make him stay.

He pulled out a chair at the table and gestured for her to sit. "How about a glass of wine?" he asked as he lit the three candles that were grouped in the center of the table.

She smiled teasingly. "Candlelight...wine...if I didn't know better, I'd believe you are trying to seduce me. All that's lacking is romantic music."

"Voilà." He flipped the switch of a boom box on the counter and soft music filled the air. "I try to cover all the bases when I'm attempting to seduce."

He cast her one of his sexy grins and she wanted to tell him mission accomplished. The power of his smile alone was all she needed to be seduced.

He poured her a glass of wine, then poured himself

one and joined her at the table. He held the delicate glass up to hers. "To fate," he said softly. "Sometimes it does something wonderfully right."

That was the beginning of a perfect night. Supper consisted of lasagna, salad and crispy bread. "I can't believe you were able to prepare all this from the time you invited me to dinner and the time I showed up on your doorstep," she observed while they ate.

He grinned, the candlelight doing dazzling things to his eyes. "I have a small confession to make. Mario's Restaurant delivers."

She laughed. "So, am I to assume that you don't cook?"

"Oh, I cook, I just don't do it very well." He sipped his wine, then continued. "I have all the patience in the world when I'm working with wood, but cooking makes me very impatient."

"I love to cook," Erica replied. "I just don't do it very often. It never seemed worthwhile to go to all the trouble just for me and Hannah. She's always satisfied with something simple like a burger or grilled cheese."

"I could be happy with a burger or a grilled cheese...if I was eating it with you."

"Oh, you're good at this seduction stuff."

He laughed. "Can you tell I'm trying really hard?"

The meal was wonderful. Their conversation was light and easy. They spoke of favorite movies, argued good-naturedly about television sitcoms, and debated the pros and cons of several social issues.

Erica found herself not only attracted to him physically, but intensely stimulated by his sharp mind and quick wit.

After dinner, they cleaned up the dishes, then Caleb set up the boom box in the empty living room and insisted they dance.

"It's like having our very own ballroom," Erica said as he pulled her into his arms. The song on the radio was a soft, almost haunting melody and the room was lit only with the candles that Caleb had moved from the kitchen table to a corner of the living room.

As they moved to the music, their bodies cast long shadows on the walls. Neither of them spoke, as if not wanting to break the spell of enchantment that seemed to surround them.

Erica had forgotten the utter pleasure that could be found in simply being held in a male embrace for a slow dance. But, as she followed Caleb's lead, her arms wound around his neck, she remembered the magic of dancing with that special somebody.

Slow dancing was an act of innocence, yet fraught with simmering possibilities as well...clothed bodies moving intimately close to a rhythm as old as time itself. Breasts to chest, hip to hip, their heartbeats raced a hundred times faster than the music.

Caleb didn't just move his feet when he danced. He moved his hips and his shoulders, as if the music didn't just surround him, but rather filled him, and in filling him, it filled her.

His hands moved languidly up and down her back,

caressing and teasing. She could feel his heartbeat, thunderously loud as it mingled with her own. His breath stirred the top of her hair, rapid breaths that spoke of rising excitement.

By the time they began their third slow dance, Erica felt as if her insides were on fire. His nearness intoxicated her and the knowledge that before long they would be making love further inflamed her.

His hands no longer caressed her on the outside of her blouse, but rather inside the cotton fabric. His warm hands moved up and down her back, occasionally wandering down to her slacks to cup her buttocks.

He dipped his head down to nibble on the sensitive skin just below her ear and she dropped her head back, allowing him to explore her neck and her throat with his hot kisses.

"You can consider me properly seduced," she said breathlessly as his mouth trailed along the line of her jaw.

"Are you sure?" He leaned back slightly to look at her, that sexy grin tilting his mouth. "I don't like to leave any job half done."

"Have you always been an overachiever?"

"Always." His mouth covered hers with heat and longing. When he broke the kiss, he swept her up in his arms. "I want you in my bed," he said.

"And I want to be in your bed," she returned.

He carried her up the stairs as easily as if she weighed less than a pound. Darkness had fallen outside and his bedroom was lit only by a stream of moonlight that danced into the windows.

He placed her feet on the floor next to the bed and instantly she undressed and crawled beneath the sheet that held his scent. He undressed just as quickly and joined her.

For several minutes they merely held each other and shared soft, sweet kisses. "We aren't going to move fast tonight. We have all night long," he said softly. He cupped her face with his hands. "You are so beautiful and being with you makes me feel so good."

His words stirred her as deeply as his touch. She remembered his toast at dinner, his remark that sometimes fate did something incredibly right. Fate had brought them together, two people hungry for love. For the first time in as long as she could remember, it seemed that fate had decided to be kind to her.

She could think no more as Caleb's hands moved over her, teasing and titillating. It was impossible to think of anything except the overwhelming pleasure his gentle touch evoked.

Before, their lovemaking had been fast and frantic, but true to his words, Caleb set the pace this time, and the pace was excruciatingly slow.

He touched her everywhere, finding erogenous zones she didn't know existed. And she returned the favor, exploring his body with her fingers and mouth.

Time stood still and everything else in the world paled except the moonlight, which grew stronger as their caresses continued.

Finally, they could stand it no longer and the need for completion brought them together in a tangle of legs and arms and hearts.

As Caleb had promised, even the actual act of love-making was agonizingly slow, achingly sweet and breathtakingly passionate. She clung to him, tears falling down her cheeks, as they rode the crest of desire together.

Sated, they remained in each other's embrace, the only noise in the room that of their breaths slowing to a more normal pace.

"Wow," he finally said, breaking the silence.

Erica laughed. "Ditto," she replied. She felt lighter, younger, more beautiful than she ever had in her life and she knew it was because of the warmth of his gaze on her.

He reached up and tucked a strand of her hair behind her ear. "It's good with us, isn't it?"

"It's better than good," she replied. She blushed slightly, not wanting to scare him away, yet wanting to tell him what was in her heart. "It feels right."

He nodded, as if he felt the same way. "I never intended this to happen, Erica." There was a soberness in his tone that suddenly sent a shiver of anxiety through her.

"What?" She fought for a lightness in tone. "You mean you never intended your seduction to lead to us being in bed together?"

His smile lingered for a moment, then was replaced by a frown. He reached out and drew a finger down the length of her face. "I never intended to fall so crazily for you. There's something we need to talk about...something I need to..."

Whatever he'd been about to say was interrupted by the shrill ring of the phone. "Let's ignore it," he said with a groan. "It's probably my well-meaning but ir- ritating sister calling to check up on me."

Erica laughed, rolled away from him and sat up. "We can't ignore it. It might be Keith. I gave him this number in case of an emergency." She reached across Caleb and fumbled for the phone. "If it's your sister, you can explain why a woman answered your phone," she exclaimed, then said hello into the receiver.

"Erica?" Keith's voice chased away any laughter that might have been left in her. "Don't panic," he said, instantly creating a wave of fear inside her. "We're at the Memorial Hospital and..."

Erica didn't wait for him to say anything further. She slammed down the receiver, already grabbing her clothes.

"Erica...who was it?" Caleb got up from the bed and reached for his jeans.

She pulled her blouse on, her fingers fumbling with the buttons. "That was Keith. They're at the Memorial Hospital."

"What happened?" Caleb grabbed his shirt.

"I don't know." She stared at him a moment, her mind blank except for one mute scream of terror. Han- nah! Her name reverberated in Erica's mind. What had happened? Dear God...was she all right? "I...I have to go. I have to get to the hospital."

"Come on." Caleb wrapped an arm around her. "I'll drive you."

Chapter 10

Caleb had never seen a woman shut herself off so effectively. As he drove Erica to the hospital, he marveled at how quickly she'd transformed from a laughing, warm, accessible woman to a tense, withdrawn, isolated one.

He reached across the seat and took her hand. It was cold, and unresponsive, neither welcoming nor avoiding his touch. Nor did she look at him, but rather kept her gaze focused intently out the front window.

Fear. Her fear filled the car. Caleb was scared, too. Scared for Hannah, scared for Erica. But he knew they had too little information to allow that fear to get blown all out of proportion.

He wanted to comfort Erica, but didn't have the words. Without knowing exactly why Keith had called from the hospital, he knew nothing he could say would provide any comfort at all.

She finally spoke, breaking the tension. "Can't you go any faster?"

"I'm driving as fast as I can," he returned. He put his hand back on the steering wheel, realizing his touch brought her no solace. It was as if she didn't know how to accept a comforting touch. "I'd rather arrive at the hospital in my car than in an ambulance following an accident."

She closed her eyes, as if suffering some enormous inner pain. "Please...just hurry."

He stepped on the accelerator, going as fast as he dared. For a moment they were both silent, the only noise the squeal of the tires as he turned corners.

"Erica," he said, needing to say something, anything that would help alleviate the tension that rolled off her. "Maybe it's something simple, not her heart at all." She didn't reply, and he continued, "Maybe Keith got sick, or Amy. It could be a dozen different things. It doesn't have to be her heart."

She turned and looked at him, her eyes drowning pools of despair. "It's not Keith or Amy, or any of their children. It's Hannah. I know it is. I feel it in my heart."

Despair ached inside Caleb. Could her mother's instinct be right? Dear God, he didn't want it to be Hannah's heart...for all the right reasons...and for all the wrong ones.

He didn't want it to be her heart because he couldn't

imagine either her or Erica having to go through the uncertainty, the fear of another bout of illness. He didn't want it to be her heart because he knew if she'd already had a heart transplant, there were few options left for her.

He adored the little munchkin and couldn't imagine the world without her in it. Finally, he didn't want it to be her heart because it was Katie's heart, and if it quit working altogether then Katie's death would mean nothing but pain.

"I should have never let her go." Erica's voice was little more than a pained whisper. "She wasn't ready. It was too much for her."

Caleb wanted to protest, but he bit the inside of his mouth, realizing now wasn't the time. When they found out what had happened, then they could sort out the rest of it.

The tires squealed in protest as he turned into the hospital lot and parked before the emergency-room entrance. Before the engine had completely shut off, they both were out of the car and running toward the hospital door.

Keith and his two daughters and son were in the waiting room. Caleb's heart jumped into his throat as he realized it was obviously Hannah who had brought them all here. Keith stood and met them as they entered.

"Where's Hannah?" Erica asked tersely.

"She's back with the doctor. Amy's with her."

Erica whirled around, obviously intent on going

through the swinging doors to find her daughter. Keith grabbed her arm and stopped her before she could take two steps.

"You didn't let me explain on the phone," Keith said with a touch of impatience.

"What happened?" Caleb asked, noting that in the fluorescent overhead lights Erica's face looked positively bloodless.

She pulled away from Keith's grip and faced him impatiently. "Explain what?"

"It's not her heart."

Erica stared at him blankly and relief soared through Caleb. "Wha..what do you mean?" Erica asked.

Keith raked a hand through his short, dark hair. "It's her chin."

"Her chin?" Erica stared at him as if he were suddenly spouting a foreign language.

"We were getting the kids ready for bed and Samantha was chasing Hannah and Hannah fell and hit her chin on the edge of the coffee table."

Tears suddenly shimmered in Erica's eyes. "Her chin?" she echoed again, visibly sagging in relief.

"I'm sorry, Erica." Keith looked miserable. "It was an accident."

"I have to go to her." Erica turned and headed for the swinging doors. This time nobody stopped her.

As she disappeared, Keith released a long, deep sigh. "One step forward...two steps back. I suppose it will probably be another six years before Hannah gets to come over to our house again to play."

"Surely not," Caleb replied. "Erica was understandably upset, but I'm sure she realizes that accidents happen when you have children."

Keith snorted. "You don't know Erica as well as I thought you did." He gestured toward the plastic chairs. "Why don't we sit."

Caleb nodded and the two men sat side by side. Nearby Keith's children were reading books, seemingly oblivious to the adults' conversation. "Once she sees that Hannah is fine, I'm sure Erica will be okay."

Keith rubbed his forehead tiredly. "I hope you're right. I feel so terrible about all this."

At that moment Amy entered the waiting room and both Caleb and Keith stood once again. "Erica is with Hannah. They're still waiting for a doctor to see Hannah. Erica says we might as well take the kids and go on home." She touched Keith's arm, a loving touch of support. "I didn't have the nerve to ask her if Hannah could come back to our house to finish out the night."

"Probably just as well," Keith replied. He dug into his pants pocket and handed Amy a set of keys. "You take the kids and go on home. I'll stay here until they finish up."

"How will you get home?" Amy asked.

"I can take him," Caleb offered.

Caleb watched as Amy kissed Keith, then Keith kissed all his kids good-night. A few moments later Keith and Caleb were alone in the waiting room. Caleb sat as Keith paced back and forth in the small confines.

"I think I'll go find some coffee," he finally said. "Would you like some?"

Caleb shook his head. "No, thanks. I'm fine."

Keith left and Caleb leaned his head back against the wall...thinking. Now that the worry about Hannah was gone, his mind whirled over the evening he had spent with Erica.

Magic. There was no other way to describe it. It hadn't been just the physical pleasure of making love to her. The magic had come from more than that. It had come from the music of her laughter, the sharpness of her wit. She stimulated him on all levels. She made him believe in life again...in love again.

One thing had become crystal clear to him this evening. As he'd taken Erica on the tour of the house, he'd realized that no matter what the future held for the two of them, the house belonged to her. Her ownership of it had been with him during every bit of work that had been accomplished.

The child's room, where he had spent so much time and attention had been for Hannah. It hadn't been a room for Katie. Katie would have wanted a canopy bed, not bunks with a jungle gym. In the back of his mind, he'd known what he was doing all along.

He also realized now that in paying for all the work to be done on Erica's little house, he'd subconsciously been preparing it for a new renter. One way or another, no matter where their relationship took them, Erica and Hannah would have their dream house.

He closed his eyes and drew a deep breath. The

scent of the emergency room touched a jarring chord inside him. He hadn't been in a hospital since the day of Katie's death. It was a smell of stale coffee and antiseptic, of blood and pain. For him it would always smell like death.

Snapping open his eyes, he stretched his arms overhead, sloughing off old memories. Tonight he was far away from the pain of his past. Tonight he was here for Erica and for Hannah.

Keith returned a few minutes later, a cup of steaming coffee in hand. He sat back down next to Caleb and blew across the top of the fragrant brew. "I got lucky. They had just made a fresh pot."

He took a sip and sighed. "I can't tell you how much bad hospital coffee I've drunk over the last six years."

"You spent a lot of time at hospitals with Hannah?"

Keith frowned. "I spent a lot of time in waiting rooms, but not necessarily with Hannah or Erica. I was there...but I don't think Erica even realized it." His frown deepened. "I was there, but she went through all of it alone."

"She doesn't have to go through anything alone again," Caleb said.

Keith smiled ruefully. "I'm not sure she knows how to do it any other way. She's a strong woman, and sometimes I think her strength is her biggest weakness."

At that moment Hannah exploded out of the swinging doors, Erica following on her heels. "Hi, Mr. Man." She raced over to him, chin raised. "Look, I got butterflies on my chin. Three of them."

"Butterfly stitches," Erica said.

"Wow." Caleb looked duly impressed. He tweaked Hannah's nose. "Guess I'd rather have butterfly stitches than elephant stitches."

Hannah giggled. "I think elephant stitches would be really, really big." She giggled again, the giggle transforming into a yawn.

"Come on, let's get you home," Erica said briskly.

"Home?" Hannah looked at her mother in dismay. "But can't I go back to Uncle Keith's?"

"Not tonight. You've had enough excitement for one night." Erica didn't look at either of the men.

"Okay, let's get out of here," Caleb said.

They were a silent group as they piled into Caleb's car. Erica sat in the passenger seat and Keith got into the back with Hannah.

"Could you take us home first so I can get Hannah to bed?" Erica asked as they left the hospital.

"Sure," Caleb agreed. Distance. It radiated from Erica. He had no idea what she was thinking, what she was feeling.

She looked tired, as if the burst of adrenaline her initial worry had produced had left her and now she was drained...exhausted. There was nothing Caleb would have rather done than put his arms around her, give her whatever support she needed, but he got the distinct impression that any touch, any means of support would be quickly rebuffed.

Her strength was her greatest weakness. Keith's words echoed in Caleb's brain. An interesting concept. Being strong and independent was commendable, but when did those qualities became faults? When you shoved away the people who loved you?

The rest of the trip was accomplished in silence. When they pulled up in Erica's driveway, Keith got out of the car as well. "Could I tuck her in?"

"Yeah, Mommy, let Uncle Keith tuck me in," Hannah said.

Erica hesitated a moment, then nodded. All four of them entered the house. Caleb and Keith sat in the living room as Erica got Hannah ready for bed. "I'm never going to live this down," Keith said softly to Caleb. "Erica is never going to forgive me for this."

Caleb looked at him in surprise. "Keith, it was an accident. No real harm done. There's nothing to forgive," Caleb exclaimed.

Keith flashed him a tight smile. "You don't know my sister. If she had her way, she'd put Hannah in a protective bubble to keep the world away."

At that moment Erica returned to the living room. "You can go on in," she said to Keith, then she moved to the window and stared out into the night.

As Keith left the room, Caleb went to stand behind Erica. He placed his hands on her shoulders, but she was as rigid as a block of stone. "Are you okay?" he asked softly.

"Of course." She whirled around, away from his touch and sank down on the sofa. "I'm fine, now that I know Hannah is fine. Thank God it was nothing more serious than stitches."

"No childhood is complete without a couple of stitches," Caleb said, but she made no reply.

At that moment Kevin came out of the bedroom. "I think she's asleep," he said. He shifted from foot to foot, his gaze intent on Erica, who was staring at the coffee table in front of where she sat. "Erica...I'm sorry about all this."

"Don't worry about it," she replied tersely. Finally she looked at her brother. "I should have followed my initial instincts and said no when you invited her to spend the night."

"Yeah, right," Keith said dryly. "I could have guessed that's what you'd say."

"Maybe I should just wait outside for you," Caleb said to Keith, uncomfortable with the conversation and the simmering tension between the siblings.

"No, please stay," Keith protested. "I have a few things I need to get off my chest, and it wouldn't hurt for you to hear them, too."

"By all means, Caleb. We have no secrets here," Erica said, a flash of anger radiating from her eyes.

Reluctantly Caleb leaned against the window frame.

"Erica, please don't do this," Keith said. He sat down next to his sister. "Please don't punish my family for an accident. Don't punish Hannah for an accident."

"Don't be ridiculous," Erica scoffed. "I'm not punishing anyone. I just think perhaps we hurried things a bit. Hannah isn't ready to spend time away yet."

Caleb felt Keith's frustration, but wisely kept his mouth shut. No matter how close he and Erica had gotten in the last several weeks, he wasn't in a position to intervene in the issues between brother and sister.

"When will she be ready, Erica?" Keith asked. "When she's ten...twenty? I think the real question here is when will you be ready?"

Erica stood up, as if not wanting to hear any more. "You just don't understand, Keith." She paced the floor in front of the sofa. "You don't understand what it's like to be afraid for your child. You don't know what it's been like for me, to have to face everything alone."

Keith stood up, took three paces to Erica and placed his hands on her shoulders. "But Erica, that's my point. You've never had to face all this alone. I was always there for you, but you never let me in." His voice radiated love and concern, and made Caleb think of Sarah and how she worried about him.

Erica's lower lip trembled, the first indication of any emotion. "You left me," she said softly.

Keith's eyes opened wide and he dropped his hands to his sides. "What are you talking about?" he asked incredulously. "Left you when?"

"First daddy left, then you did." She bit her bottom lip, as if angered by the traitorous tremble.

"I didn't leave you, Erica," Keith said emphatically. "I grew up. I was eighteen years old, it was time for me to begin my life as an adult. I didn't abandon you, I went into the army."

"It doesn't matter now," Erica said curtly and stepped away from him. "It's all water under the bridge."

"But it's not," Keith disagreed. "First Dad, then me, then Chuck." He shook his head and gazed at his sister, his love apparent in his eyes. "You think you're protecting Hannah, but it's your own heart you're trying to protect. I thought this was all about Hannah, but now I realize it's all about you."

"Oh please, stop with the psycho-babble," Erica said with the first hint of anger. "I'm making choices to protect my child."

"You might think that's what you're doing, but you aren't. For God's sake, the poor kid has an imaginary friend." Keith's voice radiated his own anger.

"It's a dream friend," Erica returned coolly.

"Same thing. It serves the same purpose, easing the loneliness of a little girl...a little girl whose mother won't let her go. The real problem here is that Hannah doesn't have a heart problem...you do." He looked at Caleb. "I'm ready to go home now." Without waiting for Caleb's reply, Keith left through the front door.

Erica stared after him, her eyes haunted. After a long moment she gazed at Caleb, the momentary vulnerable look gone. "He just doesn't understand. His children have never been sick. He's never had to hear a doctor give his child three months to live.'' She straightened her shoulders and raised her chin. "You'd better go. He's waiting for you."

"Are you sure you're all right?" Caleb asked. Keith had laid a pretty heavy load on her shoulders and he was surprised at how well she appeared to have taken it.

"I'm fine," she replied curtly.

"Do you want me to come back over after I take Keith home?" He wanted her to say yes. He desperately wanted her to need him.

"No. Really, I'm fine." She cast him an over-bright smile. "I'll call you tomorrow."

He nodded and left.

There's really no reason to feel depressed, he thought as he drove home after dropping Keith at his house. Still, he was disappointed that Erica hadn't wanted him to come back to her house.

The conversation between Keith and Erica had been illuminating in many respects. Although she'd mentioned her father leaving the family, Caleb hadn't realized the scars that each and every abandonment she'd suffered had caused on her heart. The men in her life had let her down dreadfully.

He remembered how cool she had been when he'd first met her, the icy reserve that had surrounded her like an impenetrable fortress. Protection. That's what it had been. She'd been guarding her heart against any further pain. But was it any wonder after all the desertions she'd experienced in her life?

He'd made a chink in that armor. She'd risked enough to date him, to dance with him and laugh with him. She'd allowed her guard to come down to make love with him.

But it wasn't enough for Caleb.

One step forward, two steps back. That was what Keith had said, and that was exactly what Caleb had felt with Erica this evening.

Because of a minor childhood accident, he'd lost all that he had gained with Erica. She'd crawled back into a shell of isolation, a place she considered safe for herself and Hannah...a place where there was no room for him.

He was losing her before he'd ever really had her...and damned if he knew what to do about it.

Chapter 11

The doorbell rang just after eleven on Saturday morning. "Hey Mommy, Mr. Man is here," Hannah yelled from the living room.

Damn. Erica frowned irritably. For the past four days, ever since the night of Hannah's hospital visit and the fight with Keith, Erica had managed to avoid everyone, including Caleb.

He'd called a dozen times, leaving messages on her machine. He'd come over as well, but she'd managed to pretend they weren't home and hadn't answered the door.

She heard Hannah and Caleb talking and reluctantly saved the work on her laptop, then shut off the computer. As she stood up from the table, Hannah and Caleb burst through the doorway. Hannah was riding piggyback on Caleb, her arms wrapped tight around his neck.

"Mommy, Mr. Man says we're going to a carnival," Hannah said, her dark eyes snapping with excitement.

"There's a carnival that just opened on the south side of town. It's a beautiful morning and I won't take no for an answer." Although Caleb's voice sounded strong and firm, uncertainty radiated from his eyes.

Erica didn't want to go. She didn't want to spend any time with him. She was too vulnerable where he was concerned. It was something she'd promised herself would never happen again. He frightened her because he touched her heart.

Her mind had spun in the last four days with all the things Keith had thrown at her, resulting in profound confusion about every area of her life, including her handsome neighbor...especially her handsome neighbor.

She didn't want to hurt again. She didn't think she could stand another abandonment in her life. She needed to guard her heart and withdrawing from him had been the only way she knew how.

"Please, Erica," he said softly.

"Yeah Mommy, ple-e-e-e-ase." Hannah turned the one-syllable plea into multiple syllables.

Erica wanted to be mad. After all, he should have asked her first before bringing up the carnival to Hannah. But it was impossible to maintain any sort of anger as she stared at the two eager faces, both waiting for her assent.

She threw her hands up helplessly. "I guess I'm outvoted here, so the carnival it is."

Hannah cheered and Caleb cast her a warm smile that started to clear the cobwebs that had obscured rational thinking for the past four days.

Minutes later they were all in Caleb's car, heading for the carnival that had been set up for the weekend in a shopping-mall parking lot.

"You've been avoiding me," Caleb said softly.

"I've been avoiding everyone," she admitted. "I've been doing a lot of thinking."

"And?"

She flashed him a quick smile. "And I don't think I'm ready to talk about it yet. I just want to enjoy the day with Hannah...and you."

The warmth of his answering grin created a flutter in her heart, and she wondered she had managed to get through the past four days without seeing him.

"Your wish is granted, my lady. One day of pure enjoyment with the little munchkin and me," he said.

"Mommy, look!" Hannah pointed out the window, where in the distance a Ferris wheel could be seem rising skyward. "What's that?"

"That's a Ferris wheel, honey," Erica explained. "You sit on the seats and it takes you up to the sky."

"Do you go to heaven?" Hannah asked curiously.

"No, not that high," Erica assured her. She and Hannah had shared many conversations about heaven in the past, when Hannah's future had been so uncertain.

"She's never seen a Ferris wheel before?" Caleb asked curiously.

"She's never been to a carnival before," Erica replied.

Caleb shook his head ruefully. "So many firsts she has to experience. I'm glad I get to share this one with her."

Erica knew at that moment she wanted him there to share in each and every first Hannah experienced for the rest of her life. She wanted him to be there when Hannah had her first day of school, her first date, her first child.

The past four days of contemplation had caused her to reexamine many things in her life. She'd wanted her feeling for Caleb to change. She'd been afraid to accept how important he'd become to her, afraid of being abandoned yet again.

Hannah's accident had brought back all her old fears, but now she realized it was too late for her to protect herself. Caleb was important to her. In truth, the distance of that time away from him had only crystallized in her mind how very special he'd become.

After Caleb parked the car, they piled out, instantly greeted by the cacophony of sounds and the myriad odors that belonged to carnivals everywhere.

The merry sound of a calliope battled with the excited screams of children and adults on the various rides. Bells rang, barkers shouted and laughter rose into the din.

The scents of roasting peanuts, fresh popcorn and sweet cotton candy mingled together to produce a heavenly fragrance that got digestive juices flowing and stomachs gurgling.

"Where to first?" Caleb asked. It felt perfectly natural when his hand grabbed hers, their fingers entwining as they headed down the midway.

"The Ferris wheel," Hannah exclaimed, obviously awed by the huge structure that glistened in the sunshine.

"The Ferris wheel it is," Caleb replied.

A few minutes later Caleb and Erica were safely buckled into the seat, Hannah between them, as the ride took them skyward.

"Oh Mommy, look!" Hannah pointed outward. "You can see the whole world from here," she exclaimed.

Erica and Caleb laughed. "Not the whole world, munchkin," Caleb said, "but a bunch of it."

At that moment, with Hannah's eyes shining bright with pleasure, everything that had been tumbling through Erica's head for the past four days coalesced into a single truth. Keith had been right.

Erica had been holding tight to Hannah because of her own needs, not because of Hannah's needs. She'd been hiding behind her daughter's illness, using it as an excuse to keep herself uninvolved with other people, isolated from life and love.

It was truly time to let go...time to share Hannah with the big, beautiful world. Tears misted her vision. Caleb was right. Nothing ever stayed the same and it was time to make changes in her life...in Hannah's.

Hannah deserved more, she deserved the chance to go to school, to make friends so she wouldn't have to depend on a dream friend for company.

"You okay?" Caleb stretched his arm out across Hannah's back to touch Erica's shoulder. Concern lit his eyes, making them darker than usual.

She swiped the tears from her eyes and nodded. "I'm fine. We'll talk later."

Later came when Hannah was riding one of the kiddie rides and Caleb and Erica stood on the sidelines watching. "I'm going to let her go to public school," Erica said. Caleb's arm around her shoulders was comforting and she smiled as he squeezed her closer.

"I think that's a wonderful decision. What prompted it?"

Erica smiled ruefully. "The tongue-lashing I received from my brother." Her smile faded as she thought of the harsh and emotional words she and Keith had exchanged. "For the first two days after that night, I was so angry I couldn't think straight at all. What right did Keith have to tell me how to raise my daughter, how to live my life?"

Caleb grinned at her. "The right of a brother who loves you and loves Hannah?"

"That's what I realized after I got over being mad." She looked at Hannah, who was seated in a little car shaped like a bug. Her face was wreathed in happiness and each time the car passed where Caleb and Erica stood, she waved, her giggles audible over the roar of the machinery.

"She loves life," Erica said thoughtfully. "And she deserves to live it to its fullest, and that includes disappointments and heartaches and the entire spectrum of experiences."

"My mother always told me if you don't experience the lows in life, you don't recognize the highs," Caleb observed.

"A wise woman," Erica replied. She watched Hannah and leaned into Caleb. Somehow she had the feeling that in making her decision regarding Hannah, she'd also cleared the last resistance to Caleb from her heart.

She was opened as she'd never been before to the possibility of love. But she also realized that in being that open she was also accepting the possibility of being hurt. Hurt was part of life, and in trying so desperately to protect her daughter, to protect herself from it, she'd really not been living life at all.

"You've been so strong for so long." Caleb's voice was soft and filled with admiration. "You've handled so much, all alone. Things are going to change. I want you to know that you don't have to be alone ever again."

Erica's heart expanded at his words. Never alone again. Although there was no way to guess what the future held for her and Caleb, she knew his words were true. No longer would she isolate herself and her daughter from the people who cared about them.

Yes, things were about to change. She intended to embrace all of life from now on. If she stumbled, if she got hurt, she'd pick herself up, dust herself off and start all over again. Without the fear that had been her constant companion for as long as she could remember, she found herself filled with a new hunger for everything.

As Hannah got off the ride and raced toward them, Erica grabbed Caleb's hand and smiled at him, not with just her mouth, but with her heart and soul. "Come on, let's go get a hot dog and some cotton candy. I'm starving!"

The transformation in Erica positively awed Caleb. For the first time in their relationship, he felt no reserve in her, no barriers to protect herself.

As the day progressed her laughter rang truer, her exuberance increased, and she touched him often, grabbing his hand, kissing his cheek, snuggling close whenever possible. It was as if something bad had been exorcized from her very soul, a restraint released and the end result was magnificent to see.

He'd meant what he'd told her, that she'd never have to face adversity alone again. He wanted to be at her side for everything life brought her. He wanted to share in her joys and triumphs as well as her disappointments and disillusionments.

He'd always believed he'd loved his wife as deeply,

as richly as he was capable of at that time in his life. And if Judith had lived, he would probably have been happy with her for the rest of his life.

But, Judith was gone and Erica was here, and he realized he wanted all of Erica's mornings, all of her nights, and everything in between.

As he watched Erica and Hannah riding a miniature roller coaster, his heart thudded with dread. He had to tell her the truth. Before their relationship could advance any further, he had to tell her about Katie.

The thought of her possible reaction to the news filled him with a kind of fear he'd never felt before. What if she hated him for not telling her sooner? What if she didn't understand all the reasons that had kept him silent for this long? What if she sent him away?

He was a strong man. He'd survived the death of his wife and child. But would fate decree that he suffer yet another loss? The loss of Erica and Hannah?

There's no reason to ever tell her the truth, a little voice whispered in his head. *She never needs to know about Katie and Hannah's physical connection. She never needs to know what really brought you to St. Louis and into her life.*

He dismissed the thought as quickly as it had jumped into his head. He wanted to build something lasting, something permanent with Erica, not something built on a lie of omission.

One thing was clear. He couldn't make love with her again, he couldn't ask her to make a lifetime commitment to him until he told her.

"That was fun," Hannah exclaimed as she came running over to where Caleb stood. "Did you see me and Mommy go over that big hill? Mommy screamed really loud."

Caleb laughed and picked her up as Erica joined them. "Why don't we go see if I can win you a big stuffed animal by throwing some baseballs?"

He steadfastly refused to dwell on his internal conflict today. The sun was shining too bright, Erica looked too beautiful and it was a day meant for building memories and fun, not worrying about what the future might or might not bring.

Dusk had nearly fallen by the time they were finally back in the car for the return trip to Erica's house. Hannah was sound asleep in the back seat, a large stuffed frog in her arms.

"You could have bought her a dozen of those frogs for the amount of money you spent winning her one," Erica said indulgently.

Caleb laughed, knowing it was true. "I couldn't believe my aim with a baseball could be so bad, but there was no way I was going to walk away from that booth without a frog."

Erica giggled. "I thought the guy was going to give you one just to get rid of you when you almost hit him in the head."

"There I was, trying to show off my prowess to my best girl, and I couldn't hit the side of a barn." He shook his head ruefully. "If I had any shame at all, I'd be embarrassed by my miserable performance."

He felt Erica's gaze on him, warm and tender. Her hand touched his thigh and he turned to look at her. "Is that what I am? Your best girl?" she asked, her voice slightly breathy, and sexy as hell.

"Absolutely, my best and only—and if you don't stop looking at me like that, I'll have to do something drastic," he warned teasingly.

"Looking at you like what?" she asked with feigned innocence.

"All dewy-eyed and with enough heat to melt candle wax. You wouldn't want me to pull the car over and ravish you while your daughter sleeps in the back seat."

"You're right about that. There are better places to be ravished than in a car." She removed her hand from his thigh then sighed, a sigh that filled the interior of the car with contentment. "A week ago, if you'd told me I was your best girl, I would have run for the hills. I was so afraid of being hurt again."

Dread once again rolled in the pit of Caleb's stomach. He didn't want to hurt her...ever...but he feared what revealing his secret would do to her.

"You know what's funny, I realize there are absolutely no guarantees in life, but I'm not afraid anymore. What Keith said made me reexamine so many things in my past, in my life."

"Thank God for meddling brothers. Speaking of...have you talked to Keith since the other night?"

"No. But, I intend to call him as soon as I get home."

"He loves you very much, Erica. He's hungry to be a part of your life, of Hannah's life."

"I know, and I intend to make changes that will make everyone happy. I've also decided to get a job outside the home."

Caleb shot her a surprised glance. "When did you decide that?"

She grinned. "About two seconds ago. Actually, when I realized it was right for Hannah to go to school in September, I realized that meant I could apply for a job at the paper where Sherry works."

"I think that's fantastic," Caleb said enthusiastically. He wanted her to be happy, and fulfilled, and he knew she'd only been doing the freelance work at home because it allowed her to be with Hannah.

He pulled into her driveway, shut off the engine, then unbuckled his seat belt and turned to face her. "It's amazing what six little butterfly stitches can accomplish, isn't it?"

She laughed, her eyes the color of joy. "The stitches were only the beginning. It took Keith's anger and four days of long, hard thought. In retrospect, the stitches were the easy part."

"Hannah might disagree with that assessment," Caleb replied. "Want me to carry her in?"

"If you don't mind."

It took them only minutes to get Hannah settled in bed, the ridiculous-looking stuffed frog tucked in beside her. "Good night, munchkin," Caleb said as he gently kissed her forehead.

"''Night Mr. Man,'' she replied, half-asleep. "I love carnivals and I love you."

The words sang through Caleb's soul, finding every dark space that had ever existed and filling him with light. "I love you, too, munchkin," he replied softly.

And he did. He loved Hannah for all the things she was and all the things she was not. He loved her strength of spirit, her tomboy ways, her brown hair and brown eyes. He loved her for the distinctive person she was, loved her in spite of the fact that he saw nothing of his own child in her.

Together he and Erica left Hannah's bedroom and went into her living room. "I'd better head home," he said, walking toward the front door.

"You don't have to hurry off. In fact...you could stay the night...if you want." The invitation shone in her eyes, the promise of desire sated, passion spent. However, he knew the invitation meant far more than a simple desire for lovemaking.

The two previous occasions when they had spent intimate time together they'd been alone. Hannah hadn't been in the house, sleeping in her bedroom.

By offering the invitation now, Erica was inviting him not only in her bedroom, but also into her life and her daughter's life. She was allowing the last barrier to drop between them.

The temptation to stay was enormous. Caleb could easily imagine awakening in the morning with Erica in his arms. It was also easy to visualize Hannah's surprise and delight when she discovered her "Mr. Man" had spent the night.

As much as Caleb wanted to take her up on her offer, he couldn't. It hadn't been that many hours ago that he had promised himself no more making love to Erica until he told her the truth.

There was nothing he'd have liked more than to blurt it all out immediately, finally get it over with and face the consequences now. But, it didn't seem fair to destroy the happiness she'd claimed for herself today. Tomorrow. Tomorrow he'd tell her.

He walked over to where she stood and drew a finger down the side of her face. "There's nothing I'd rather do than stay with you...but I can't. At least not tonight. I've got some things I need to take care of," he improvised. "And you mentioned that you wanted to talk to Keith."

He leaned down and captured her lips with his, putting all his love, all his emotion into the kiss. "Another night," he whispered as he released her.

She smiled and nodded. "Maybe tomorrow night. And that reminds me...tomorrow evening about five, I'm planning a little something special. Could you come over then?"

He shrugged. "Sure. Can you be more specific?" he asked curiously.

"It's a secret." Her eyes danced merrily. "And you know what they say about secrets...if they're shared, then they aren't secrets anymore."

"Okay. Five o'clock tomorrow. I'll be here." Together they stepped out on the front porch and shared a final, lingering kiss.

Tomorrow night, after her "something special" and after Hannah was in bed, he'd tell her everything, he vowed as he stepped off her front porch.

"Good night, Caleb," she called after him.

He turned and looked at her for a long moment, wanting to hold forever in his mind, in his heart, the picture of her with love shining from her eyes and happiness glowing on her face.

"Erica, whatever the future brings, I want you to always remember I love you." He didn't wait for her reply, but turned and hurried to his car.

As he started the car and moved it into his own driveway, he wondered if when he told her about his connection with Hannah she'd remember the words he'd just spoken and cling to the love that had blossomed between them. Or would she cut him out of their lives forever, effectively destroying any hope for happiness they might have had?

Chapter 12

He loves me. Caleb's words rang joyously through Erica's heart. She'd felt his love, had seen it shining from his eyes, but nothing compared to actually hearing the words from his lips.

She rode a cloud of happiness back into her house and sank down on the sofa, allowing the exhilaration of Caleb's love to wash over her, through her.

He loved her, and he loved Hannah, and she couldn't imagine how things could get any better, how her future could look any brighter.

Thank goodness Keith had knocked her upside the head with his words. Thank goodness he'd made her reexamine what she'd been doing, how she'd been handling her life and Hannah's. If he hadn't, then Caleb's declaration of love would have scared her away.

For the first time in years, she felt as if everything in her life was falling into place, coming together in positive terms. For the first time in years, she wasn't dreading what tomorrow might bring.

Hannah was healthy and it was time mother and daughter each took wing just a little bit and explored what they could become both together and separately.

And the very next time she saw Caleb, which would probably be first thing in the morning, she intended to tell him she loved him. She shivered with pleasure. Strange to think that two months ago she wanted nothing to do with him, and now she couldn't imagine doing without him.

She reached over and picked up the phone. The first person she intended to call was Sherry, to find out if the job at the newspaper was still available. The second person she wanted to call was Keith.

She'd been unconsciously punishing him for years because he'd left home soon after their father had gone. She'd viewed his leaving with a child's perception and had been caught in deep feelings of abandonment. She'd done a lot of growing in the past four days, and it felt wonderful.

An hour later she hung up the phone after talking to her brother. Peace eddied through her. A lot of healing had occurred in the last forty-five minutes with him. They had talked about their father's abandonment, how differently it had affected each of them. For Keith, he hadn't been able to wait to get out on his own and become the father his own hadn't been.

Although Keith had been eighteen when their dad had left, his memories of the time when his dad had still been in the home weren't pleasant.

In talking through all of it with him, Erica had realized she, too, had unpleasant memories of the cold, distant man she'd desperately wanted to love her. The end result was a fear of being hurt by all men, including the one she had married.

Poor Chuck. He'd never really had much of a chance with her. She'd been too young, too afraid to truly give her heart. It had been far easier for her to devote herself to Hannah and the health problems. Although she wasn't willing to accept all the blame for the marriage that had ended. Chuck hadn't really wanted to stay. Hannah's health problems had scared the hell out of him.

As she got into bed, she was at peace. It frightened her just a little...how wonderful life suddenly felt. When she drifted off to sleep, it was to sweet dreams of Caleb and love and happily-ever-after.

She awakened late the next morning, surprised to find Hannah still in bed and sleeping soundly. The excitement of the carnival the previous day had obviously worn them both out.

Dressed for the day, she padded into the kitchen and made a pot of coffee. When it was ready, she carried a cup out the back door and sank down at the picnic table, her gaze going across the expanse of the yard to Caleb's house.

Was he still sleeping? Out running errands? Perhaps

conducting his business by phone or by fax? What had kept him from spending the night last night?

She smiled, recognizing she sounded like a woman in love. Sipping her coffee, she hoped he looked out his window and saw her sitting here. She'd made a full pot, anticipating him joining her. She was eager to see him, eager to say those three magical words to him.

I love you. She closed her eyes as sheer pleasure traveled through her. It had been a very long time since she'd said those words to anyone other than Hannah. She couldn't wait to say them to Caleb.

She was on her second cup of coffee when Hannah wandered outside. Still clad in her pajamas and rubbing her eyes sleepily, she crawled up on Erica's lap.

"You're getting so big," Erica said softly, enjoying the pleasure of holding the little girl who was growing way too fast.

"I'm big enough for lots of things now, aren't I, Mommy?"

"Yes, you are," Erica replied. "You're even big enough to go to real school when it starts in September."

Hannah sat up and stared at her mom, her eyes wide. "For real? I can ride the school bus and have a backpack and everything?"

Erica laughed. "Yes. You can ride the school bus and maybe today while we're out running errands we can get you some supplies and a backpack."

"Oh goody!" Hannah clapped her hands together

with excitement. "Tell me what else. Tell me more about school."

"Well, you'll get to learn all kinds of new things, wonderful things, and I'll be your room mother."

Hannah frowned. "What's a room mother?"

"I'll come to school sometimes on special occasions and bring cupcakes and cookies and we'll have a little party with all your friends."

"Can Mr. Man be a room dad?"

"I don't think Mr. Man bakes cupcakes," Erica said, fighting a smile of pleasure at the very thought.

"No, but he could build everybody a tree house." Hannah looked inordinately pleased at the idea.

Erica laughed. "You'll have to talk to Mr. Man about that."

Hannah nodded. "When can we leave to go get my supplies?"

"As soon as you get dressed." Before the words were completely out of her mouth, Hannah hopped off her lap and scurried into the house to get dressed for the day.

Once again Erica's gaze went to Caleb's place. There were no movements at any of the windows, no evidence that he was even home. Maybe he'd had early morning errands, or a business problem that required his attention.

She smiled as she thought of Hannah's plans for Caleb as a room daddy. A tree house for every student—only Hannah would come up with such an idea.

Erica finished the last of her coffee, then reluctantly

went back into the house. Surely if Caleb was home and available for coffee, he would have come over by now.

"Mommy, I'm ready." Hannah raced into the kitchen, Peaches at her heels. "Let's go get some school stuff."

"Okay." Erica grabbed her keys and a few moments later they were off.

The day flew by far too fast. Erica had no idea buying a backpack would be such a big deal, but it turned out to be a major mission.

Hannah had definite ideas about exactly what she wanted, the color...the material...how many pockets and zippers. It took four stores before they found the one that Hannah proclaimed perfect.

They bought notebook paper, crayons, pencils and glue. When they had finished with the supplies, Erica decided to buy Hannah a new outfit for the first day of school. One outfit grew to four. Although it was still a little over a month away before the school year would begin, she knew that if she got the job at the paper, time would pass far too fast.

From the stores, they drove to a tree nursery. "Why are we buying a tree?" Hannah asked curiously as Erica paid for the small Bradford pear tree.

"It's a secret," Erica replied. "You'll find out later today."

As the tree was loaded into the back of her car, Erica looked at her watch, surprised to see that it was nearly three o'clock. Where had the day gone?

When they got back home, Erica was vaguely surprised to find no phone messages on the machine from Caleb. After the day they'd spent together yesterday and his parting words the night before, his silence felt oddly disturbing.

Stop obsessing, she chided herself. He had no way of knowing that she was eager to see him, excited to profess her love for him. He was a businessman. He had a life separate from hers. He'd said he'd be here at five for the surprise.

However, when five o'clock came, Caleb didn't. Keith and Amy and their children arrived, filling the house with noise and laughter.

Hannah instantly took the two girls into her bedroom to show them her new school clothes and supplies, leaving little Billy to wrestle with his mother for control of the floral centerpiece in the middle of the coffee table.

As Erica prepared soft drinks for everyone, Keith joined her in the kitchen. "We brought something for Hannah," he said.

Erica looked at him in surprise as he held out a gold necklace with a heart locket. Keith grinned. "Did you really think I didn't realize that exactly a year ago today Hannah got her new heart? That's what this little celebration is all about, isn't it?"

"Yeah." She smiled at Keith. "It's hard to believe it's been a whole year. In some ways it feels like only yesterday and in other ways it feels like a lifetime ago."

Keith picked up the tray of drinks. "Where do you want to go with these?" he asked.

"Backyard." Within minutes everyone had been moved outside. The kids played tag in the yard and Keith, Amy and Erica sat at the picnic table.

Again and again Erica's gaze went from her watch to Caleb's house; she couldn't stop wondering why he hadn't shown up yet or at least called.

By six, she knew she had to go on with her plans, with or without Caleb. Keith helped her dig the hole for the new tree, then they all gathered around as Erica helped Hannah lower it into place. All the kids helped put the dirt around the base of the tree. When it was firmly set, Erica stepped back and placed a hand on Hannah's shoulder.

"We planted this tree to mark the first anniversary of Hannah's heart," she said. "Exactly one year ago today Hannah received the heart that gave her life." To Erica's surprise, tears sprang to her eyes. She laughed with embarrassment and hastily swiped them away.

As Keith presented Hannah the heart necklace, Erica fought the rising emotion inside her. Exactly a year ago, she'd believed her daughter wouldn't live through the remainder of the day. And then, a miracle occurred. The doctor came into Hannah's hospital room and told her a heart was available.

Erica had asked no questions. She hadn't wanted to know where the heart had come from, or why it was now available. All she wanted to know was if the doctor thought the transplant would work. Would it save her daughter's life?

Now, Erica found her head filled with questions. She knew the heart had belonged to a child, and that somewhere a mother and father were grieving the loss of their beloved daughter or son.

She didn't like to think about this aspect of the transplant operation, that one had died so another could live, that her happiness was based on somebody else's tragedy.

Hannah's excited chatter broke into Erica's thoughts. "Mommy, Uncle Keith says if it's okay with you, I could spend the night with them tonight."

"He did?" Erica looked at her brother.

"And I promise, no stitches this time," Keith said.

"I'll move the coffee table into the garage," Amy added.

Erica laughed. "Okay, if you're sure?" She looked from Keith to Amy.

"We're sure," Amy replied. "The girls love being with Hannah and what's one more in this brood?"

By seven, Erica was alone in the house. She washed up the last of the dishes, then put on a fresh pot of coffee. Why hadn't she heard from Caleb? As the minutes of the day wound down, his silence grew more ominous.

She poured herself a cup of coffee and went to stand at the kitchen window. She looked over to Caleb's house, surprised to see his kitchen light shining out into the dusk.

So he was home. Why hadn't he come over for the celebration? Why hadn't he called her? She frowned worriedly. This wasn't like him. This wasn't like him at all. Concern fluttered through her as she wondered exactly what was going on.

Caleb had a hangover. He swallowed two aspirins, poured himself a cup of fresh coffee and sank down into a chair at his kitchen table.

He should be shot for starting the morning drinking beer. He'd never been much of a drinker, but the moment he'd opened his eyes that morning and remembered what day it was, he'd thirsted for anything that would dull his senses, take away the pain. A year ago today he'd lost his Katie.

Pain. Grief for the child he'd lost, but that wasn't the only source of his pain. Although he would always miss his daughter, his heart had accepted her death and the passing of time had eased that particular ache.

No, it was the anguish of guilt that gnawed at his gut, seared through his soul. If only he'd stopped the car on that fatal morning. If only he'd taken the time to insist that Katie sit down and buckle up.

And now an additional burden of guilt lay like a block of cement in his chest. Last night, after leaving Erica's home, after telling her he loved her, he'd been struck by the depth of his deception where she was concerned.

He loved her with every fiber of his being, and he knew she had grown to love him just as deeply. But what chance did love have when it was based on a lie? She had no idea what had brought him here, to St. Louis, to her. And his lie of omission weighed heavy on his soul.

He had come to St. Louis not as a businessman in need of a vacation, but rather as a grieving father seeking peace, looking for answers.

Some of those answers, he had found. He knew now there was no essence of Katie Rose McMann inside Hannah Marie Clemmons. He had stopped looking for his daughter in Hannah's every gesture, every word, every expression. The answers to that particular question had brought him a kind of peaceful closure.

However, the questions he had concerning his future with Erica had not been answered. He feared those answers. He'd watched from the window as she and her family had planted the tree. He'd known from the moment he'd opened his eyes that morning, the moment he'd realized what day it was, that Erica's secret had to be a celebration of Hannah's heart transplant.

He'd desperately wanted to share in that celebration, but couldn't. He hadn't belonged there, not with the truth of his own secret burning in his stomach.

He jumped as the doorbell rang. Who in the hell could that be? But he knew who it was. He'd known all along that if he didn't show up today, didn't at least call her, she'd come to him. He also knew that she wouldn't leave tonight without knowing about Katie, about Hannah and what had brought him to her.

Wearily he walked through the living room, then

opened the front door. Her loveliness caused a bitter-sweet ache inside him. The loving concern on her face would have been a balm to his spirit if he wasn't so tormented by what he had to tell her.

"Caleb…are you all right?" she asked. She stepped inside the door and instantly placed a hand against his cheek, as if checking for a fever. "Are you ill?" He knew he probably looked it…sickness of the spirit could ravage a man.

He took her hand in his and pulled it away from his face, finding her gentle, loving touch almost physically painful. "I'm not sick…at least not physically."

"When you didn't show up this evening at my place, and didn't call or anything, I got worried. Are you sure you're okay? You don't look well at all."

He nodded and pulled her toward the kitchen. "Come in and sit down, Erica. We need to talk. There are some things I need to tell you."

He saw a slight shimmering fear in her eyes, as if she sensed the conversation to come might be unpleasant. She sat at the table and he pulled up a chair next to hers.

"You aren't going to tell me you're married, are you?" She stiffened as if preparing herself for outrage.

"No…no, I'm not married," Caleb hurriedly replied. He raked a hand through his hair, then rubbed his stubbly jaw, desperately trying to figure out how to tell her what he needed to say.

"Caleb…what is it?" She laid a hand over his, her touch achingly warm.

He drew a deep breath. "You told me once that I'd make a good father. I am a father, I mean I was a father for seven years. Her name was Katie Rose McMann and she died in a car accident."

"Oh, Caleb," she gasped, her shock obvious. Instantly she leaned forward and wrapped her arms around him. He found no solace in her attempt to comfort him.

He stood, forcing her to release her hold on him. Again he drew a hand through his hair and walked over to lean against the sink counter. "We were driving in the car, running late as usual. Katie was in the back seat, being stubborn and refusing to put her seat belt on."

When he closed his eyes, the vision of the morning drive that had so often haunted his dreams unfolded before him. "I should have stopped the car. I should have pulled over to the side of the road and not driven a mile further until she was safely buckled in."

Katie's sweet voice filled his head. "I love you, Daddy Doodle." He shoved aside her voice and continued his story. "A semi crossed the center line. I didn't have time to react, to avoid the crash." He heard the tension in his voice. "Katie probably would have survived if she'd been wearing her seat belt." These last words blew from him as if carried on a forlorn wind.

"Caleb, you can't do that to yourself. If anyone was at fault, it was the truck driver who crossed the line.

You can't blame yourself for the accident. And you can't blame yourself for a tragedy.''

"Then who do I blame?'' It was a rhetorical question and he didn't expect an answer from her.

She stood and walked over to him. Wrapping her arms around his neck, she leaned into him, as if to share what she assumed was his grief.

For a long moment they held each other. He could feel her heartbeat mingling with his own, felt the empathy that rolled off her in waves.

Hope buoyed him. Maybe she'd understand after all. Maybe she wouldn't be angry with him, wouldn't cut him out of her life.

"You want to see a picture of Katie?'' he asked. He hoped that if he could make her see his Katie, know sweet Katie, then she'd understand the overwhelming forces that had driven him here, in search of Katie's heart.

"Sure,'' she agreed and stepped back from him.

He pulled out his wallet and flipped it open, then withdrew the picture of Katie he always carried with him. It was a second-grade school picture, and one that captured her little-girl essence perfectly.

He handed the photo to Erica and watched as she studied it. "She's beautiful,'' Erica said softly.

For the first time all day Caleb felt a smile curve his lips. "She was beautiful. She loved ribbons and dolls and tea parties.''

"And you.''

Emotion choked in his throat as he nodded. "And me."

"Caleb, why didn't you tell me about her before?" Erica searched his face. "I can't tell you I know the pain of losing a child, but I can tell you I know the fear of losing one." She placed her hand on the side of his face, her gaze filled with love.

"You've given me such happiness, you should have known you could share this pain with me. I love you, Caleb. I want to share all of it with you...the joys and the pains of life."

He allowed the words she'd just spoken to wash over him in a flood of warmth and pleasure. How he had wanted to hear those words from her...but after...after he'd told her everything.

He drew a deep breath, knowing the time had come. It could not be put off any longer. "Erica, the car accident that claimed Katie's life occurred exactly one year ago today. Katie died, but I agreed that her heart would be donated for transplant." He watched her eyes widen as comprehension dawned. "Erica, my Katie's heart now beats in Hannah's chest."

Chapter 13

"What?" She stared at him. She thought she'd heard what he said, but wasn't certain. It couldn't be what she thought she'd heard.

"Katie's heart…Hannah has it now."

"Is this your idea of a tasteless joke?" Erica's head reeled with the echo of his words.

"No, it's the truth."

She recoiled and stepped back from him, an overwhelming sense of betrayal assaulting her from within, creating an anger that momentarily stole her breath away.

"Erica, please…let me explain."

"Explain what?" Her anger found her voice. "That you came into my life and my daughter's life under false pretenses? That you lied about everything just to gain some sort of access to me and Hannah?"

"But that's not true," he protested and took a step toward her.

"Stay away from me," she warned him, appalled to feel the sting of tears in her eyes. She swiped at them angrily. "I thought you loved me, loved Hannah, but I know now your love is as phony as everything about you. My God, I can't believe this. All you wanted was to replace the family you lost. That's what this has all been about all along."

"That's not true!" He held his hands out in a gesture of helplessness. "For God's sake, please listen to me. Let me explain everything."

Erica drew in a deep breath, desperately trying to gain control of her anger and the pain that swirled inside her heart. "Just tell me one thing…how did you find us? The doctors at the hospital actively discouraged me from trying to find out anything about the donor, which wasn't a problem for me because I didn't want to know anything."

He frowned, looking more weary, more ill than he had when Erica had first arrived. "The day of the accident, after I'd agreed to donate Katie's heart, I overheard a nurse say that it was going to St. Louis."

He leaned back against the refrigerator, as if too exhausted to stand without support. "For months, I did nothing about it. I threw myself into my work, hoping that would help me cope." He rubbed a hand across his forehead, his fingers pausing to momentarily massage one temple. "It didn't help. Nothing helped. So,

I contacted a private investigator to help me find the child who had received Katie's heart.''

A private investigator. A paid informant. A stranger had delved into her life, offering Caleb the pieces he'd found. Had he told Caleb all about the poor divorced woman with the sick child? Had he told Caleb about their financial struggles, how she lived her life? A sense of violation mingled with the betrayal.

''Why?'' She felt as if she were about to break into a million pieces. ''What on earth did you hope to accomplish by coming here, by meddling in our lives?'' she asked, still angry but needing to understand.

He pushed off from the refrigerator and walked across the kitchen floor to take a seat at the table. ''Please...sit. If I could just explain why I came here, why I needed to connect with you and Hannah, then maybe...you'll forgive me.''

She didn't want to sit with him, she didn't even want to be talking to him. Pain ached inside her, the pain of love lost, of dreams forsaken. At the moment, forgiveness seemed way out of the question.

There was no way she could believe that he truly loved her. He loved the heart that beat in Hannah's chest, his daughter's heart. And he'd convinced himself that he loved Hannah's mother. How nice and neat. How utterly convenient.

No, she didn't want to hear anything he had to say...and yet knew she couldn't leave here without knowing what it would be. Without volition, unable to stop herself, she took the seat opposite his.

"When I first decided to come here to St. Louis, I just wanted to see Hannah, make sure she was healthy and doing okay." His eyes were a deep, midnight color, as if the silvery starlight in them had been momentarily banished by thoughts of his daughter's death.

He averted his gaze from her and stared out the nearby window, where only the darkness of the night was visible. "I thought it would be enough, to drive by and get a glance of her. I thought it would be enough, but it wasn't."

He looked at her once again, the silver glow back in his eyes, but so intense it nearly stole her breath away. "If, at any time before the moment of Katie's death, I had been asked my thoughts about the human heart, I would have replied that the heart is nothing but a pump necessary for life. No magic, nothing mystical about it."

"But your opinion changed?" she asked, despite the fact she told herself she didn't care why he'd come, why he'd manipulated his way into their lives.

He leaned back in his chair and dragged a hand through his dark hair, a gesture she recognized as a sign of his nervousness, his agitation. "No, my opinion didn't necessarily change, but I did begin to wonder about possibilities."

"Possibilities?" She wasn't sure she understood. She wasn't sure she wanted to understand. How had this happened? How had everything gotten so crazy and mixed-up?

"Poets write about the heart, we talk about people being heartsick, heartbroken, kindhearted and on and on." He leaned forward, and Erica smelled the familiar scent of him, the clean maleness that had wrapped around her each time they made love.

She wanted to weep because she knew she'd never have that experience again. Never again would she allow him to hold her in his arms, kiss her lips, or work his magic on her heart. He was leaving her heart as he'd initially found it. Dead...empty...lonely.

"Erica, I had to find out for myself if the heart remembers...if the memory of the people loved, the experiences shared are indelibly written into it. I had to find out if any of the essence of Katie, any of her memories, her likes and dislikes, any piece of her love for me still lived in her heart, inside Hannah."

"And did you get your answer?" Erica asked stiffly, trying desperately to refuse to be moved by the stark, deep emotion that shone from his eyes.

"Yes." He shrugged. "The heart is just a pump, nothing more...nothing less."

Erica stared down at the top of the table. "I'm sorry you didn't find what you were looking for," she said softly.

"Oh, but I did."

She looked at him with surprise.

He smiled, the intensity in his gaze gone. "I came here looking to heal, for closure, and I found that. I will always miss my daughter and there will always be a piece of my heart that aches with her loss, but

I've also come to a place of peace where she's concerned.''

"I'm glad for you." And she was, but that didn't change the fact that she knew there was no chance of a future for the two of them.

"I didn't come here looking for love, but I found that, too." He tried to take her hand in his, but she pulled away, his touch killing her. "Erica, I swear I didn't mean to deceive you."

"But you did." Didn't he see how deeply the deception had hurt her? How it had made everything else they'd shared a complete and total lie?

"Yes, I did," he agreed wearily. "I made some bad decisions, but they were made for all the right reasons. At first, I didn't tell you who I was and what my connection to Hannah was because I was afraid you'd see me as some sort of psycho nutcase and send me away."

"But it was my right to make that decision." She stood and took several steps away from the table, unable to stand his nearness any longer.

"I know that." He stood as well, his expression pleading with her. "I didn't tell you because I was afraid, because I was slowly falling in love with you and didn't want it to end."

"So, why did you decide to tell me now?" she asked bitterly. "Why not just keep this information to yourself forever?"

"I couldn't do that. I couldn't do it because I want

to marry you, I want to build a life with you, and I didn't want that life to rest on a lie.''

Anguish once again pierced through Erica. An hour before this moment, she'd believed they were on their way to sharing their lives. She'd believed in his love and had anticipated a proposal of marriage sometime in the near future.

Now his words felt like nothing more than a cruel taunt. She'd made the foolish mistake of believing that Caleb had been sent by fate to right all the wrongs that had happened in her life. All she heard at the moment was a roaring in her ears, the sound of fate's heartless laughter.

She couldn't stay any longer, couldn't stand the sight of him. He'd lied. Every time he'd held her, every time he'd loved her, it had been a lie.

''This wasn't right, Caleb. This isn't right,'' she said.

He walked toward her, arms opened as if to embrace her, but dropped his hands to his sides when he saw her stiffen. ''Erica...maybe what brought me here was an unhealthy impulse, an irrational need to find answers nobody will ever know. But, what has kept me here is my love for you. It's the one real, true, right thing that's come out of all this.''

He took her by the shoulders, his fingers squeezing gently. ''Don't walk away from me, Erica. Don't walk away from what we have. You have to believe me when I say I know exactly what's in my heart for you and for Hannah. I know Hannah is not my daughter and I know that you are the woman I love. There is no confusion in my head where either of you are concerned.''

She spun away from his touch, hurt and anger overwhelming her. ''But I don't believe it. I can't believe it, and even if I did, how do I get past the fact that my gain is because of your loss?'' She drew a shuddery breath. ''I don't want to see you again, Caleb...and I don't want you to see Hannah anymore.''

The tears she'd tried so desperately to hold back filled her eyes as she turned and ran for the back door.

''Erica.''

His anguished cry didn't slow her down. She flew out of the house and into the night, deep, wrenching sobs tearing from her throat. Half-blind with tears, she stumbled through the gate that led to her yard.

Damn him, she thought. Damn him for not telling me sooner. When she reached her own door, she looked backward, grateful that he hadn't come after her.

For a moment, her mind stamped with the image of his silhouette in the doorway, shoulders slumped in utter aloneness. Someplace in the dark recesses of her mind, she knew it was an image that would forever haunt her.

The house was deadly silent around her as she sank down into the corner on the sofa and drew her knees up to her chest.

Heartache. How long had it been since she'd experienced it? How long had it been since she'd felt as if a deadly arrow had pierced her heart? She couldn't remember ever feeling this kind of pain.

His child. Katie Rose McMann. A vision of her picture swam in Erica's head. A beautiful little girl with golden-blond hair, bright blue eyes and a sweet smile. In the photo Erica had seen, Katie had been wearing bright pink ribbons in her long hair and she'd looked like a little fairy princess.

A fairy princess who was dead. And no kiss from a handsome prince would awaken her from her forever sleep. Erica squeezed her eyes tightly closed, trying to dispel the vision of the child.

She hadn't wanted to know this. She hadn't wanted the donor heart to have a name…a face. She had tried to pretend the heart came from heaven, without any grief attached, without any loss connected to it.

Hannah lived because Katie Rose had died. Erica's happiness was built on Caleb's grief. She couldn't look in his eyes without seeing the image of his daughter, without feeling the pain of his loss.

Erica couldn't understand why her heart had finally been healed only to be broken once again by Caleb's love and his loss.

He'd gambled and lost. On the evening of the third day since she'd stormed out of his house, Caleb stood at his window, staring at the tiny house behind his.

There had to be some way to make Erica understand

that his love for her and for Hannah had nothing to do with what he'd lost. It had everything to do with what he'd found with her.

He'd told her the truth when he'd said that he'd finally come to terms with Katie's death…at least as well as a father could ever come to terms with the loss of a child. He'd found peace within himself and felt no need to create a Katie from a Hannah.

The only real need he had was for Erica. Erica, with her bright blue eyes and lustrous hair. Erica, with a warrior's courage and the musical laughter of an angel.

He spent long hours staring at her house, but in the three days since his confession, there had been no sign of Erica or Hannah.

The waning sunlight cast deep shadows on the tree house. Without Hannah, it appeared abandoned, and he wondered if the structure would ever again ring with the sound of her infectious laughter.

In a million years, he never would have built a tree house for Katie. She'd have much preferred a doll-house with intricate staircases and sweeping balconies.

How could he make Erica realize that there was no confusion in his mind? The day of Hannah's birthday celebration, when he'd bought the inappropriate gift of a doll for her, he'd successfully separated the two girls in his mind and in his heart. He'd known then that Katie was gone, but that he could love this child of Erica's, he could love Hannah for herself alone.

He straightened his shoulders, hope sweeping through him as Erica's back door opened and she emerged. She didn't just walk to the gate that separated the two properties, but stalked, her footsteps short and quick. In her hand she carried a bundle of papers.

She was angry. He felt it radiating from her as she slammed the gate behind her and approached his back door. As she drew closer, he saw the twin spots of color that dotted her cheeks. Red. The color of anger.

"Caleb McMann, you open this door," she shouted at the same time her fist beat a wrathful tattoo on the door frame.

He opened the door, knowing instinctively what had set her off. At least he'd have another chance to talk to her.

"I can't believe you did this," she exclaimed. She brushed past him and into the kitchen, then turned and glared at him. "What are you trying to do? Buy me? Buy Hannah?" She threw the handful of papers on the table.

Caleb didn't have to look at the papers to know what they were. He'd had them drawn up by a lawyer the previous day. "Of course I'm not trying to buy you," he replied.

"You can't just give us a house," she protested indignantly. All he could think of was how lovely she looked, with anger snapping in her eyes and coloring her cheeks.

"Why not?"

"Because....because it just isn't done," she sputtered.

"Of course it's done." He eyed her hungrily. He ached with the need to wrap her in his arms, hold her tight, love her forever. "Parents buy their children homes, divorcing couples give each other houses."

"You aren't my parent and we aren't married."

"But we could be." His words made the color in her cheeks intensify and she averted her gaze from him. "Erica, the house was refurbished specifically for you and Hannah. Each piece of wood that was sanded, every wall that was repaired was done with the two of you in mind. This is your dream house and it wouldn't be right for anyone else to live here."

"You should sell it and use the extra money to get therapy," she replied.

He laughed. "I don't need therapy, and even if I did, I have more money now than I'll ever use in a lifetime."

She eyed him suspiciously. "Of course. I should have seen it all along. Stanley didn't suddenly become a generous benefactor, did he? You paid for all the repairs. You paid for the central-air unit and the painting and everything."

He shrugged. "I wanted you and Hannah to be comfortable. It was no big deal. And I don't want to sell this house."

The spots of color in her cheeks were fading, leaving her pale and tired-looking. "I can't accept the house, Caleb. It wouldn't be right. If you don't want to sell it, then you live here."

"I can't do that." He stared at her intently, wanting

her to feel the waves of love that emanated from him. "I can't stay here and feel you and Hannah so close, see the two of you out in your yard, know you're getting on with your life and I'll never be a part of it. I love you, Erica, and I can't live here knowing there will never be a future for us together."

Her eyes closed for a moment, but not before he saw the hint of desire, a flame of wistful longing.

He took a soundless step toward her, then another one, and her eyes snapped open as if she'd sensed his approach. "Erica, do you really think Hannah is so unlovable that I couldn't love her for the child she is, completely separate from my daughter? Do you really think *you* are so unlovable that I couldn't have come here and fallen completely and utterly in love with you?"

She looked at him with eyes that showed no emotion whatsoever. "Did you really think you could come here and lie about everything and somehow it would all work out okay? Did you really think this wouldn't make a difference?" She turned and headed for the door. "I won't take the house, Caleb. Talk to your lawyer and get that deed changed." With these words she disappeared back outside.

Chapter 14

"Mommy, are you and Mr. Man mad?" Hannah asked as Erica tucked her in that evening.

"Why do you ask?" Erica smoothed the dark hair away from Hannah's sweet little face.

"'Cause we haven't seen Mr. Man in forever." Hannah's dark eyes studied her mom thoughtfully. "Friends can disagree and still be friends," she said, parroting Erica's words from the day they'd had lunch with Sherry.

"I know that, honey, but it's a little more complicated than that."

"Everything is compicated with you," Hannah exclaimed with a sniff of indignation. "You won't get married and you won't get me a baby brother or a sister 'cause it's too compicated. I don't like compicated."

Erica smiled, leaned over and kissed Hannah's forehead. "Get some sleep, Hannah. Things will be okay in the morning."

Hannah nodded, but not before Erica saw a glimmer of tears in her bright, dark eyes. "What's the matter, honey? What's making you sad?" Erica asked, afraid she knew the answer.

"My dream friend," Hannah replied, a fat tear trekking down her cheek.

Erica looked at her in surprise. She'd been afraid Hannah was going to tell her she missed Caleb. "Your dream friend? Why is she making you sad?"

Another tear played tag with the first, racing down Hannah's little cheek. "She's going away."

"Going where?"

Hannah shrugged. "I dunno. She didn't tell me that. But, she told me last night in my dream that she was gonna have to go away soon." Hannah's face scrunched up and a little sob escaped her. "I don't want her to go. She's my bestest friend."

"Oh, honey." Erica pulled Hannah into her arms and held her tight as Hannah cried. As Erica patted her daughter's back and made soothing mommy noises, she thought about the irony of the situation.

For months...for years, she'd been careful to keep people who might abandon them away. She'd wanted to protect Hannah from the loss of somebody she loved. But, she'd never dreamed her child would suffer the abandonment by an imaginary friend. How did a mother guard against that? And when does that kind of protection become destructive?

"Shhh," Erica soothed, suppressing the tears that burned at her own eyes. Tears for Caleb. Tears for Katie. Tears for all of them.

It had been three days since she'd last spoken with Caleb, three days since she'd seen him, three days that felt like a lifetime. When did the hurt stop? Did it ever really stop?

Hannah cried for several minutes, then Erica got her settled back beneath the sheets. "You know what I think?" she asked as she used a tissue to dry the last of Hannah's tears.

"What?" Hannah asked.

Again Erica smoothed Hannah's hair away from her face. "I think your dream friend knows it's time to say goodbye to her because you're going to make so many other, wonderful, real friends when school starts."

"Really?" Hannah eyed her hopefully. "You really think I'll have lots of friends?"

"Tons," Erica replied. "I think you'll have so many new friends you won't have time for a dream friend any longer. Maybe your dream friend needs to go visit another little girl while she sleeps, a little girl who has no real friends."

Hannah nodded, her eyes heavy with the need for sleep. "And I'll find a real bestest friend, one that doesn't like to play with dumb old dolls. That would be nice," she said. "Good night, Mommy."

Once again Erica kissed her forehead, then crept toward the door. "Mommy?" She turned back to look at Hannah. "You should get glad with Mr. Man again instead of being mad and sad with him. He'd make a good daddy. He has daddy eyes." With these final words, Hannah fell asleep.

Erica padded into the living room, trying not to think about Hannah's words. She didn't want to think about Caleb McMann. She'd spent the last several days doing nothing but thinking of him, loving him, and mourning what might never be.

She moved from the living room to the kitchen and stood in the darkness, staring out the window at his house.

Her house.

She couldn't believe he'd given her the house. When she'd opened the papers from the law firm, she'd looked at them in bewilderment before comprehension dawned and she realized what Caleb had done.

He'd given her a dream—in a million years, she never would have been able to possess a house like that.

How many times had she stood at this very window and coveted the house? Even with all its wrinkles and warts, the house had represented a complex dream… one that, she now realized, involved much, much more than a mere building.

Feeling the sting of tears, she left the window and went back into the living room, where she curled up on the sofa. Every time she had thought of owning that house, the vision had been accompanied by dreams of herself, and Hannah, and a special man that would make them a real family.

Caleb. Thoughts of him ached in her heart. She realized that without Caleb, there was no dream. He was the man she had dreamed about. In the darkest hours of the night throughout the past six difficult years, she had longed for him, prayed for him, needed him.

On those nights, he'd had no face, no name, but she knew now that it had been thoughts of Caleb McMann that had kept her going, kept her strong, kept her fighting throughout Hannah's illness.

Now he was offering her not only his house, but his love and his heart as well, and she couldn't take any of them. She closed her eyes, trying desperately not to think of him.

One thing was certain. The entire experience, throughout her time with Caleb, her heart had opened in ways she hadn't thought possible. She now realized that every day, in every experience she'd shared with Hannah before Caleb, her insidious fear had somewhat dulled the joy of life. That wouldn't happen again. Never again would she give fear such power over her.

She didn't know how long she sat, ruminating, contemplating, aching with her thoughts when Peaches pounced up on the sofa, her little pom-pom tail wagging happily. "Hey Peaches, what's going on?" Erica asked as she scratched the poodle behind an ear. Peaches rolled over on her back, encouraging Erica to scratch her plump belly. Erica frowned, absently stroking the soft fur. "What are you doing out here?"

Peaches rarely left Hannah's bedroom once the little girl was asleep. She'd curl up on the end of Hannah's bed, like a little guardian angel watching to make certain her miniature mistress stayed safe.

Finding the poodle next to her sent a flutter of disquiet through Erica. She stood and headed for Hannah's room, wanting to check to make sure she was okay.

As she entered the room, the first thing she noticed was the opened window with the screen dislodged. The second thing was the empty bed.

"Hannah?" She turned on the light, hoping the illumination would prove her initial vision wrong. But it didn't. Erica reeled with alarm and flew from the bedroom. Stumbling down the hall, she cried out for Hannah several times, even knowing as she did with a mother's instinct that the child wasn't in the house.

She raced out the back door of her house, crying out in the darkness of the night. Where had Hannah gone? What had happened? Panic surged inside her.

Hannah had been peacefully sleeping when Erica had left her room. They'd had no fight, no argument of any kind. Why would Hannah run away? Dear God...*had* she run away?

Erica stared at the dislodged screen and open window and a new thought chilled her to her bones. Had somebody else opened the window? Dear God, had somebody taken Hannah?

"Hannah!" Her terrified cries brought Caleb to his back door.

"Erica, what's wrong?" He left his house and hurried toward the gate. She met him there.

"Hannah's gone. She apparently went out the window and now I can't find her."

Simultaneously, they both looked toward the tree house. A flutter of relief coursed through Erica. "Of course," she murmured. "I should have thought of that."

Caleb opened the gate to let Erica through and together they walked to the base of the tree house. "How long has she been gone?" Caleb asked.

Erica frowned and looked at the luminous dials on her watch. "I'm not sure. About a half an hour or so."

"Did you two have an argument? Was she in trouble?" he asked.

Erica shook her head. "Not at all. Everything was fine. She was in bed and asleep the last time I saw her."

Caleb looked up the ladder. "She probably climbed up there and promptly fell asleep. I'll go up and get her."

Erica stood at the foot of the ladder as Caleb climbed up. She intended to have a long, hard talk with her daughter about the fact that windows weren't supposed to be used as escape routes.

Her anxiety rose to near panic as Caleb descended the ladder without Hannah in his arms. "She isn't there," he said once he was back on the ground.

"Are you sure?" Erica reached out and grabbed Caleb's hand. "Then where is she? Where could she have gone? We have to call the police." She heard the hysteria in her voice, felt it clawing up the back of her throat.

Caleb wrapped an arm around her shoulder, a thoughtful frown on his face. "Let's not panic. There's one other place she might have gone."

"Where?"

"Come on." He led her to his back door. "The last time Hannah ran away, she came here. My door has been unlocked all evening. It's possible she came in and I wasn't aware of it."

"I just don't understand this at all," Erica said, tightening her grip on Caleb's hand. "Why would she sneak into your house?" As they entered the kitchen, Erica didn't care why Hannah might have come to Caleb's house, she only hoped Hannah was indeed there.

"If she came in here, I think I know where she is," Caleb said. Still holding hands, the two of them went up the stairs and down the hallway. They stopped in the doorway of the bedroom with the bunk beds, and there she was, sound asleep on the top bunk.

Erica walked to the side of the bed and stared for a long moment at the sleeping child. Slowly, her heartbeat returned to a more normal pace.

"Hannah?" She touched the child's shoulder and Hannah stirred and opened one sleepy eyelid.

"Hi, Mommy. I comed to Mr. Man's house to sleep."

"Yes, I know. Why did you do that?"

"'Cause my dream friend told me to." Her eyelid fluttered shut and Erica knew she was once again sleeping soundly.

Erica left the bed and rejoined Caleb in the hallway. "I don't understand this at all. Why would she come here? Why would her dream friend tell her to come here to sleep?"

Caleb gazed at Erica, his eyes radiating that silvery glow that sent a shiver of delight and a sliver of pain through her. "Hannah knows she belongs here, that this room is hers." He took her hand once again and pulled her down the hallway, where their voices wouldn't disturb the sleeping child. "She knows that room was designed specifically with her in mind, just like the rest of the house was designed specifically with you in mind."

"Caleb..." She tried to pull her hand from his, but he held tight.

"There's nothing more I can do to make you see how much I love you. There's nothing left to say that will make you understand that I'm not a man driven to replace what I've lost, but rather a man who found the unexpected gift of love. I love you, Erica, and I know you love me, too."

"I do." The words whispered from her. "I do love you, Caleb. But I can't stand the thought that Katie Rose had to die so Hannah could live. I can't stand the thought that you had to lose your child so I could keep mine."

"Oh Erica, that's not the way it is at all." He dropped her hand and instead placed both his palms on the sides of her face, forcing her to gaze at him.

"Katie Rose died. Nothing I could have done, nothing you could have done, could have stopped that from happening. She was dead whether Hannah got her heart or not. What the doctors did by placing Katie's heart in Hannah's chest was to make Katie's death count for something. They made it mean something good. Without that, Katie's death would have been for nothing and we'd both be grieving the loss of our daughters."

Erica stared at him, his words whirling around and around in her head. For the past several days, since he'd told her who he was, all she'd been able to focus on was the fact that Katie had died so that Hannah could live. Now, the truth of the situation struck her. Katie had died...and Hannah had lived. But, even if Katie's heart had not been placed in Hannah, Katie still would have been dead.

Tears spilled from Erica, and as Caleb wrapped her in his loving arms, she wept. She cried for Katie, for Caleb, and with her tears came a cleansing of her spirit. She realized that all along she'd needed to mourn the little girl whose death had given Hannah the opportunity to live.

When the tears were gone, there was nothing left inside her, nothing but love for Caleb. His heart had become hers, his soul had intricately wound around hers, making it impossible for her to think of a life without him in it.

"Are you okay?" he asked softly as she swiped away the last of her tears.

"I'm more than okay," she replied. She didn't make a move to step out of his embrace. Rather, she leaned her head against his chest, listening to the sound of his heartbeat as it whispered softly to her own.

"I accept the offer of this house. I want to live here, raise Hannah here, but my acceptance comes with a condition," she said.

"A condition?" She heard his heartbeat thudding faster.

Tilting her head back, she looked up at him. "I won't live here unless you live here, too. I want you with us, forever and for always."

The sparkle of a million stars lit his eyes. "Are...are you sure?"

She smiled. "I've never been more sure of anything in my entire life."

She barely got the words out of her mouth before his lips possessed hers, as if to brand her as his forever.

"Marry me, Erica," he said as their kiss finally ended. "Please marry me and let me love you every day for the rest of my life."

"Yes," she said, a surge of joy welling inside her. "Yes, yes, yes!" She laughed, but the laughter was stilled as his lips once again found hers in a kiss that left no doubt as to whether he loved her or not. As her arms wound tight around his neck she knew she held her dreams. Finally, for the first time in her life, fate had finally gotten it right.

Epilogue

Caleb watched with loving indulgence as Erica tied Hannah's hair bow for the third time in fifteen minutes.

"Hurry, Mommy. The bus is gonna come and I don't want to miss it on the very first day of school," Hannah exclaimed. The excitement of the big day glowed in Hannah's cheeks, shone from her eyes. She was even more excited about school than she had been about Erica and Caleb's wedding the week before.

"Okay...okay, I'm finished," Erica said.

"How do I look?" Hannah asked first her mother, then turned to grin at Caleb. "Do I look like a first-grader? I don't want to look like I'm in kindergarten."

Erica stepped back and surveyed her daughter with a critical eye. "You look at least six...maybe seven years old," Erica replied, and Caleb thought he heard a catch of emotion in his wife's voice.

He placed an arm around her shoulders and gave her a tight squeeze, knowing this day was as difficult as they got in the parenting arena. "I think you look like my little munchkin," Caleb replied and was rewarded by one of Hannah's infectious giggles.

"Come on, we'd better get out there. The bus will be here any minute." Erica hurried them all outside to stand on the sidewalk in front of the house. "You have your lunch money?"

Hannah patted her pocket. "Yup."

"And you know if you need me for anything during the day you can go to the nurse's office and call me," Erica said, a worried frown creasing her forehead.

"Mommy, it's okay," Hannah said, then smoothed the plaid skirt she wore. "I'm going to be just fine."

At that moment the school bus lumbered around the corner, bringing with it the smell of exhaust and the sound of children laughing.

"It isn't a big yellow monster ready to eat your child," Caleb said into his wife's ear.

She laughed, the frown disappearing from her forehead. "I know."

"And the minute Hannah gets on that bus, I know just what we can do to take your mind off worry." Caleb watched Erica's eyes deepen and a slight blush color her cheeks. God, he loved this woman.

"You're insatiable," she whispered.

He grinned. "Only for you."

With a squeal of brakes, the bus stopped before them and the doors whooshed open. With a grown-up little wave over her shoulder, Hannah climbed up the stairs and disappeared into the bus. A moment later she appeared at an open window. "'Bye, Mommy, I love you!" she yelled. "And I love you, too, Daddy Doodle." The bus pulled away.

A piercing sweetness swept through Caleb even as his mind worked to tell him it had just been a coincidence, a crazy fluke. As the familiar words echoed in his head, he decided not to speculate, not to wonder where they had come from.

"Caleb?" Erica looked at him worriedly. "Are you all right?"

"Yes...yes, I'm fine." He looked at Erica, his wife...his love, and decided nobody really knew or understood the ways of the heart and perhaps nobody was meant to. Some things were truly better left a mystery.

Beneath a newly planted tree in their backyard was a marker that read: In Loving Memory of Katie Rose and In Celebration for Hannah's Heart. Two little girls...one big heart, and in the entwining of their lives, Caleb had learned one true thing. The heart knew love, and his was overflowing.

* * * * *

Coming this July,
Silhouette Intimate Moments welcomes you
back to the lively western town of

MUSTANG, MONTANA

in IMMINENT DANGER—the next installment
in Carla Cassidy's engaging miniseries. Will
passion and peril bind a vulnerable beauty and
a strapping sheriff together...forever?

INTIMATE MOMENTS®

Silhouette®

and

BEVERLY BARTON

bring you more riveting romantic stories in
the exciting series

THE PROTECTORS

Ready to lay their lives on the line, but unprepared for
the power of love

Available now:
MURDOCK'S LAST STAND
(Intimate Moments #979)

Available in July 2000:
EGAN CASSIDY'S KID
(Intimate Moments #1015)

Look for more books in THE PROTECTORS series in 2001!

Available at your favorite retail outlet.

And don't miss these past Protectors titles, which you can order now:

DEFENDING HIS OWN, #670, 10/95
GUARDING JEANNIE, #688, 1/96
BLACKWOOD'S WOMAN, #707, 4/96
ROARKE'S WIFE, #807, 9/97
A MAN LIKE MORGAN KANE, #819, 11/97
GABRIEL HAWK'S LADY, #830, 1/98
KEEPING ANNIE SAFE, #937, 7/99

Silhouette®

Where love comes alive™

If you enjoyed what you just read,
then we've got an offer you can't resist!

Take 2 bestselling
love stories FREE!

Plus get a FREE surprise gift!

SILHOUETTE'S 20TH ANNIVERSARY CONTEST
OFFICIAL RULES
NO PURCHASE NECESSARY TO ENTER

1. To enter, follow directions published in the offer to which you are responding. Contest begins 1/1/00 and ends on 8/24/00 (the "Promotion Period"). Method of entry may vary. Mailed entries must be postmarked by 8/24/00, and received by 8/31/00.

2. During the Promotion Period, the Contest may be presented via the Internet. Entry via the Internet may be restricted to residents of certain geographic areas that are disclosed on the Web site. To enter via the Internet, if you are a resident of a geographic area in which Internet entry is permissible, follow the directions displayed on-line, including typing your essay of 100 words or fewer telling us "Where In The World Your Love Will Come Alive." On-line entries must be received by 11:59 p.m. Eastern Standard time on 8/24/00. Limit one e-mail entry per person, household and e-mail address per day, per presentation. If you are a resident of a geographic area in which entry via the Internet is permissible, you may, in lieu of submitting an entry on-line, enter by mail, by hand-printing your name, address, telephone number and contest number/name on an 8"x 11" plain piece of paper and telling us in 100 words or fewer "Where In The World Your Love Will Come Alive," and mailing via first-class mail to: Silhouette 20th Anniversary Contest, (in the U.S.) P.O. Box 9069, Buffalo, NY 14269-9069; (In Canada) P.O. Box 637, Fort Erie, Ontario, Canada L2A 5X3. Limit one 8"x 11" mailed entry per person, household and e-mail address per day. On-line and/or 8"x 11" mailed entries received from persons residing in geographic areas in which Internet entry is not permissible will be disqualified. No liability is assumed for lost, late, incomplete, inaccurate, nondelivered or misdirected mail, or misdirected e-mail, for technical, hardware or software failures of any kind, lost or unavailable network connection, or failed, incomplete, garbled or delayed computer transmission or any human error which may occur in the receipt or processing of the entries in the contest.

3. Essays will be judged by a panel of members of the Silhouette editorial and marketing staff based on the following criteria:

   > Sincerity (believability, credibility)—50%
   > Originality (freshness, creativity)—30%
   > Aptness (appropriateness to contest ideas)—20%

   Purchase or acceptance of a product offer does not improve your chances of winning. In the event of a tie, duplicate prizes will be awarded.

4. All entries become the property of Harlequin Enterprises Ltd., and will not be returned. Winner will be determined no later than 10/31/00 and will be notified by mail. Grand Prize winner will be required to sign and return Affidavit of Eligibility within 15 days of receipt of notification. Noncompliance within the time period may result in disqualification and an alternative winner may be selected. All municipal, provincial, federal, state and local laws and regulations apply. Contest open only to residents of the U.S. and Canada who are 18 years of age or older, and is void wherever prohibited by law. Internet entry is restricted solely to residents of those geographical areas in which Internet entry is permissible. Employees of Torstar Corp., their affiliates, agents and members of their immediate families are not eligible. Taxes on the prizes are the sole responsibility of winners. Entry and acceptance of any prize offered constitutes permission to use winner's name, photograph or other likeness for the purposes of advertising, trade and promotion on behalf of Torstar Corp. without further compensation to the winner, unless prohibited by law. Torstar Corp and D.L. Blair, Inc., their parents, affiliates and subsidiaries, are not responsible for errors in printing or electronic presentation of contest or entries. In the event of printing or other errors which may result in unintended prize values or duplication of prizes, all affected contest materials or entries shall be null and void. If for any reason the Internet portion of the contest is not capable of running as planned, including infection by computer virus, bugs, tampering, unauthorized intervention, fraud, technical failures, or any other causes beyond the control of Torstar Corp. which corrupt or affect the administration, secrecy, fairness, integrity or proper conduct of the contest, Torstar Corp. reserves the right, at its sole discretion, to disqualify any individual who tampers with the entry process and to cancel, terminate, modify or suspend the contest or the Internet portion thereof. In the event of a dispute regarding an on-line entry, the entry will be deemed submitted by the authorized holder of the e-mail account submitted at the time of entry. Authorized account holder is defined as the natural person who is assigned to an e-mail address by an Internet access provider, on-line service provider or other organization that is responsible for arranging e-mail address for the domain associated with the submitted e-mail address.

5. Prizes: Grand Prize—a $10,000 vacation to anywhere in the world. Travelers (at least one must be 18 years of age or older) or parent or guardian if one traveler is a minor, must sign and return a Release of Liability prior to departure. Travel must be completed by December 31, 2001, and is subject to space and accommodations availability. Two hundred (200) Second Prizes—a two-book limited edition autographed collector set from one of the Silhouette Anniversary authors: Nora Roberts, Diana Palmer, Linda Howard or Annette Broadrick (value $10.00 each set). All prizes are valued in U.S. dollars.

6. For a list of winners (available after 10/31/00), send a self-addressed, stamped envelope to: Harlequin Silhouette 20th Anniversary Winners, P.O. Box 4200, Blair, NE 68009-4200.

Contest sponsored by Torstar Corp., P.O. Box 9042, Buffalo, NY 14269-9042.

ENTER FOR A CHANCE TO WIN*

Silhouette's 20th Anniversary Contest

Tell Us Where in the World You Would Like *Your* Love To Come Alive... And We'll Send the Lucky Winner There!

Silhouette wants to take you wherever your happy ending can come true.

Here's how to enter: Tell us, in 100 words or less, where you want to go to make your love come alive!

In addition to the grand prize, there will be 200 runner-up prizes, collector's-edition book sets autographed by one of the Silhouette anniversary authors: **Nora Roberts, Diana Palmer, Linda Howard** or **Annette Broadrick**.

DON'T MISS YOUR CHANCE TO WIN! ENTER NOW! No Purchase Necessary

Silhouette®
Where love comes alive™

Visit Silhouette at www.eHarlequin.com to enter, starting this summer.

Name:

Address:

City: State/Province:

Zip/Postal Code:

Mail to Harlequin Books: **In the U.S.**: P.O. Box 9069, Buffalo, NY 14269-9069; **In Canada**: P.O. Box 637, Fort Erie, Ontario, L4A 5X3